The Larmand Family
Oct - 71
from
Aunt Irene & Uncle Tom

A Touch of Jonah

A TOUCH OF JONAH

A Father Bredder Mystery Novel

BY LEONARD HOLTON

DODD, MEAD & COMPANY
NEW YORK

Library of Congress Catalog Card Number: 68-23091
Printed in the United States of America

A Touch of Jonah

One

"FATHER," said Barbara Minardi, "will you be angry if I ask you a sort of very personal question?" She was helping him weed one of the flower beds in the garden of the Convent of the Holy Innocents, a task for which she had volunteered for two reasons. The first was that she liked Father Bredder, who was concerned about the growth of weeds in the flower beds. The second was that she was hoping in this last week of the semester to earn extra credit which would raise her flagging grade in biology.

"Go ahead," said Father Bredder, at peace with all the world because for the first time in four years his dwarf orange, in a tub by the door of the rectory, showed definite signs of producing ripe fruit. He was from Ohio, and one of the ambitions of his life was to grow at least one orange in California.

"Well," said Barbara, who at sixteen was becoming aware of some of the many dialogues in the world. "Is it true that by next year all priests have to marry?"

"Heavens!" cried Father Bredder, shocked completely out of his oranges. "Whoever put that idea in your head?"

"Janie Parks said it's part of the modernization of the church. A priest can't be modern unless he has a wife. And children. You know. He can't know about the problems of married life unless he's married."

"In the same way, I suppose," said Father Bredder, "that a doctor can't know anything about leprosy unless he is a leper. Though," he added hastily, "I don't mean that leprosy and marriage are the same thing."

"Do priests really know a lot about marriage?" asked Barbara. "I mean how can they—when they're not married themselves? I mean quarrels and things. And you know —Other women." Barbara had known Father Bredder since infancy and so was accustomed to talking quite as openly with him as with her own father, Lieutenant Louis Minardi, whom she didn't get to talk to as much as she wanted, since he was a policeman and subject to the most erratic hours. He worked in Homicide.

"Yes," said Father Bredder. "We do. You see, Barbara, what goes wrong in marriage first of all goes wrong inside a human being—a man or woman. Marriage is only a state, though a very important one. And a wrecked marriage is only the outward sign of a wrecked soul, usually wrecked by selfishness. Whenever a husband or a wife puts his or her interest first, then a marriage is in danger. Selfishness kills love. Even in business . . ." He stopped. "I'm giving you a sermon," he said. "I'm sorry. What I wanted to say was that you don't have to know about marriage to be a priest—but only about human beings and their relationship to God."

"So you don't have to get married next year?" asked Barbara.

"Certainly not," said Father Bredder, with rather more emphasis than was necessary.

"That's good," said Barbara with genuine relief. She had uncovered a pale fat grub in her weeding and was now poking it with a stem of grass. Probably, she thought, she ought to kill it. It looked like the kind of thing that might eat Father Bredder's oranges. On the other hand she didn't like killing things, not even horrid fat grubs. She picked it up gently on the stem of grass and hurled it away, calculating that it would take the grub four weeks to find its way back to the orange tree, and by that time the oranges would be ripe and plucked.

"I'm glad I'm not God," she said. "All those decisions."

"What decisions?" asked Father Bredder.

"Oh, grubs and oranges. Which is more important? But never mind. You're quite sure that priests don't all have to get married next year?"

"Quite sure," said Father Bredder.

Barbara sighed with deep satisfaction. "That's good," she said. "You know a woman needs a man she can take her troubles to and doesn't have to keep her eye on at the same time."

Then she was gone, leaving Father Bredder a little bemused by the perceptiveness of the female mind at sixteen. He mentioned the matter at lunch to his assistant Father Armstrong, an English priest with a doctorate in literature from one of the Oxford colleges.

Father Armstrong was not even slightly surprised. "Women are not really cleverer than men," he said. "What is taken for cleverness is merely the result of passivity. Where the male is active, the female is contemplative and cunning, and as a result spends far more time thinking over patterns and problems, and so on. Women are, as it were, oriental—men occidental."

At that moment Mrs. Winters, the housekeeper, entered briskly with a tray to clear away the luncheon dishes. She was a small woman, but plump and fiftyish, and she wore at all times a black straw hat on her head, giving the impression that she had just arrived in a great hurry or was just about to depart in an equally great hurry. Father Armstrong believed that the hat was a symbol of independence—Mrs. Winters' notice to the priests and to the world that she could quit at any moment.

"You didn't eat your dumplings," she snapped at Father Armstrong. "That's a waste and sinful."

"Too hot for dumplings," said Father Armstrong.

"That's no excuse," said Mrs. Winters. "I made them special and now they will be wasted." She glanced at Father Bredder's plate. Father Bredder had eaten all his dumplings, but out of pure cowardice, knowing Mrs. Winters' temperament. She sniffed. "See," she said. "Father Bredder has eaten all of his and he's bigger than you. You'll never be big like him unless you eat well."

"My dear Mrs. Winters," said Father Armstrong. "Growth, physical size, is a matter of genes rather than appetite."

"It's a matter of eating," said Mrs. Winters and, having scattered the findings of the geneticists to the winds, she swept out with the loaded tray.

"Oriental?" asked Father Bredder with a smile.

"God's exception to man's rules," said Father Armstrong. He eyed his superior with affection and yet with a measure of appraisal. It would be hard to find thrown together two men of wider background speaking the same language as their native tongue, he mused. Father Bredder was of country American stock—from Twin Oaks, Ohio. Although the priest was only in his early fifties, he belonged to an America that was receding rapidly into the past, an

America of hickory and corn and leafy lanes, careless summer flowers, wild plums and horse-powered farms—though
Father Armstrong reflected that in Father Bredder's youth
tractors were already lumbering over the rich American
prairies, plowing or harvesting. Still there was a kind of
strength from early rural America in the big frame of
Father Bredder, in his essential kindness and simplicity
which were not at all to be confused with idiocy.

He, Father Armstrong, was of the English aristocracy
—of people who had had money in quantity as a right
through a score of generations. There were an Armstrong
coat and an Armstrong manor house and an Armstrong
Park to this day. His father, Viscount Yalloden, still, at
seventy, occupied the hereditary seat in the House of Lords
and sent him an occasional letter which read like an order
and was always written on the familiar deep blue paper
with at the top a crest depicting an arm holding a mace.

Different indeed, and yet, since both were priests, the
same in their essentials. Contrasting their backgrounds in
this manner, Father Armstrong was reminded of something
vaguely unpleasant.

"I had a letter from On High this morning," he said.

"On High?" echoed Father Bredder. "You mean the
Bishop?"

"No, the Viscount—my father," said the other. "He has
never been able to understand that my duties to the priesthood come before my duties to the family. He thinks of my
being a priest as the same sort of thing as Hugh, my
brother, being in the army—something to pass away the
time. Leave can be obtained from the army to shoot pheas-
ants in September or attend Ascot in May. And leave can

be obtained from the priesthood to go to Hawaii since the family relationship or obligations demand that this be done."

"Hawaii?" echoed Father Bredder. Hawaii was the last place he would associate with Father Armstrong.

"I'll read you the pertinent part of the letter," said the other. He produced several sheets of blue paper, riffled through them and said, "Here we are. I quote, as the columnists say 'In July, Stockton is sailing *Fair Maid of Fowey* to Honolulu in the Transpacific Race, and I expect you to go with him. In fact, I have told him that you will go and it is important that you should for other than personal reasons. Since you keep telling me that you have taken this vow of poverty (what the devil for? Aren't there enough poor people in the world? Don't you understand that the wealthy are there to encourage the poor to greater effort?)—I have given Stockton a thousand or so for your expenses. Contact him at the Newport Beach Yacht Club, which I think is somewhere near Los Angeles, though I recall visiting a Newport that was in a place called Rhode Island some thirty years ago. Still, there are probably two of them. The race starts on July 4th which I think is some kind of a national holiday in your part of the world.

" 'I had a stern word with Willsden the other day on the coal . . .' Oh, well, the rest is politics."

"By Willsden does he mean the Prime Minister of Great Britain?" asked Father Bredder.

"Yes," said Father Armstrong. "The old man still thinks the Peers should direct the Commons. And he continues to do his best in that direction."

"You could very easily get leave to go to Hawaii in July," said Father Bredder with a tone of envy. "School will have closed for the summer. And you need a vacation."

"I'm going to take one, too," said Armstrong. "But not on Sir Harry Stockton's whacking great yacht. I'm going to spend the summer at the Huntington Library researching Fletcher. There's an exciting little pocket of uninvestigated papers on Fletcher at the Huntington."

"You mean the contemporary of Shakespeare?" asked Father Bredder.

"Precisely," said the other. "I will be voyaging on far more exciting seas than those traveled by the *Fair Maid of Fowey*. You know there was a play by Fletcher and Shakespeare, the pages of which Warburton's cook used to start a fire with. . . ." He went on, but Father Bredder was soon lost in a maze of Elizabethan and Jacobean playwrights.

He was very pleased to have such an exciting assistant, and his admiration for Father Armstrong was deepened. Peers, yachts and Elizabethan playwrights. What a glittering variety. Against such a background his own raising of oranges in a tub was quite insignificant.

"I've never seen a big yacht," said Father Bredder. "Nothing more than a punt we had on a little lake at home."

"Then you shall go on one," said Father Armstrong. "I'll call Sir Harry and we'll go down and view the *Fair Maid of Fowey* together. It will give me a chance to tell him in person that I can't come. Consider it done."

That afternoon Father Bredder spent a little while musing over a globe of the world in the sitting room of the rectory. He turned the globe to the California coast and picked up the tiny dots two thousand miles or so distant that represented the Hawaiian Islands. What an adventure—just what he had dreamed of many a time poling the leaking

· 7

punt along the shore of the little lake in Twin Oaks. He caught for one moment the smell of mud and wood associated with the punt and then fancied that he heard the roar and hiss of breakers on a coral reef and the seething of a trade wind through pandanus and palm. Father Armstrong, entering the sitting room quietly, caught Father Bredder dreaming before the globe and said softly, "Yo ho ho and a bottle of rum."

"Just boyhood," said Father Bredder, blushing.

"Yes," said Father Armstrong gently. And he quoted from the Mass: " 'I will go to the altar of God; to God who gave me the joy of my youth.' "

Two

SIR HARRY STOCKTON was seated in a bosun's chair at the top of the 85-foot mainmast of the *Fair Maid of Fowey* admiring the view, though he had gone aloft to inspect personally the spinnaker block and shackle. Below him was spread out the impressive yard of the Southland Boat Works. In the center was a turntable on which yachts and fishing vessels, pulled out of the water on a marine railway, could be turned and shunted off to different work areas. The turntable, circular and gray, looked like the center of some curious flower whose petals were the weathered lines of track which radiated outwards from it. His own boat, though 72 feet long, was utterly dwarfed by his feet dangling below him. It amused Sir Harry to discover that he could cover the yacht from transom to bow with one foot, obliterating between heel and toe an expenditure of some three quarters of a million dollars, which was what the yacht had cost him.

The duraluminum mast, from whose top in the bosun's chair he now dangled like a fly in a spider's web, had cost twenty thousand pounds—about sixty thousand dollars—and that was without any of its winches, rigging, or other fittings. He thought it rather too heavy and was considering getting a new one, in which case his present mast would be junked—it had no resale value at all.

There were several other yachts in the yard below him, all fitting out for the Transpacific Ocean Race (called the Transpac) from San Pedro to Honolulu. There was the 70-foot sloop *Mistral* of Bennington's which had an aluminum hull and was, to Sir Harry's mind, basically a 70-foot sailing dinghy. There was Ted Wirth's redoubtable ketch *Gesture,* designed by the famous Herreshoff and built in 1925—boat for boat perhaps the fastest of them all, though she was quite hopeless in a light wind. And there was a scattering of Cal 40s and Cal 50s, one of which would undoubtedly win the Transpac on corrected time, for the handicap system made it quite impossible for a big yacht to win.

The big yachts competed more for the honor of being first to finish—of being first to burst past the buoy off Diamond Head, perhaps at night, to be caught, lovely as an angel, in the searchlight that marked the finish line after dark, and to receive the acclamation of the thousands of Hawaiians who waited, often for days, for the first of the Transpac boats to come in from the ocean.

Fair Maid of Fowey was a completely new boat. She had not been raced before, which was one reason that Sir Harry was himself checking the details of her rigging. The riggers employed at the yard were experts, but Sir Harry liked to check everything himself. This, he felt, kept everybody on his toes, and while among yacht racing men it was considered an honor to crew for Sir Harry Stockton, a berth on his yacht meant unending work and constant vigilance. Sir Harry would tolerate no slackness.

Looking over the top of the sheds around the yard, Sir

Harry could see an arm of Los Angeles Harbor running up to the Watchorn Yacht Basin on his right. The yacht basin bristled with the masts of sailboats. To his left the harbor opened up, the water flat behind the breakwater, but ruffled by a brisk wind in the area called Hurricane Gulch, where a thirty-knot wind blew each afternoon through a slot in the surrounding hills. Beyond the breakwater, interrupting the horizon, lay the island of Santa Catalina, at this distance looking like two blue islands because of the isthmus dividing it. A hundred miles beyond Catalina was the real ocean—the powerful rolling immensity of the Pacific, which was the proper place for his yacht to be; out in the ocean wind, away from the petty breezes and spiteful storms of the land.

"Ten days, I should say," Sir Harry said to himself, estimating for the hundredth time the period required to sail from San Pedro to Honolulu. "Ten days, which would be about two hundred and fifty miles a day, which means only an average of a little more than ten knots. Certainly ten days. Perhaps nine and a bit like *Big Ti* in 'sixty-five, if we get heavy winds." And he looked out beyond Catalina, his thin nose raised a little, like a dog's scenting the wind.

He didn't like the spinnaker halyard block. It was a light-weight block of stainless steel, custom-made for the ship (as indeed were all the fittings of the *Fair Maid*). But the cheeks of the block had thin edges which, though rounded, still provided a potential source of trouble. A halyard pressing against the cheek of the block with a strain on it of several tons might be cut through. Using a marlin spike, Sir Harry unshackled the block, put it in a canvas bucket tied to the seat of the bosun's chair, and signaled the deck that he wanted to come down.

"Get rid of that block," he said to the head rigger who met him at the base of the mast. "And get rid of all the blocks like it on board."

The head rigger was a slow-moving man who seemed to be bursting out of his clothes. His face was red, which increased the sense of pressure, and the redness of his face was emphasized by his white hair. He stood well over six feet and seemed to have to reach down to take the block from Sir Harry. He looked it over carefully, subjecting it to the analysis of his own mind.

"What's wrong with it?" he asked.

"It has one overwhelming fault," said Sir Harry. "I don't like it. So get rid of it. And all others of the same kind. Replace them with standard Crittendens of equal size."

The head rigger turned to a man standing at his elbow. "You heard," he said. "Get on with it. And you"—pointing to another—"tell the storekeeper to get in fifty four-inch Crittendens, thirty-eight . . . Here. I'll give you a list."

He turned to Sir Harry. "It may take a day or two to round up all we need," he said.

"Put six men in taxis and send them to every marine store in San Pedro if necessary," said Sir Harry. "And don't bother me with your problems. I want the *Maid* back in the water ready to sail tomorrow. Can you manage that, John?"

John Samuels, manager of the yard, gave him a little smile. "Tide will be right at nine-thirty," he said. "We can do it." He wondered whether to add that this would mean keeping two crews working through the night, but decided against this. Sir Harry never quibbled about money—only about getting his own way.

"Fine," said Sir Harry, and glared about him so that the men who had collected around faded away, leaving him to get out of the bosun's chair himself—a task which gave him a little difficulty, for he had to use his pliers on the snap shackle. He then made his way aft toward the big but shallow cockpit of the *Maid*. The decks of the yacht were littered with every kind of marine store—coils of rope of all sizes, amounting to small hills; other coils of flexible stainless steel wire; mounds of sail bags and other mounds of food in cans and jars and plastic containers; crate upon crate of these, and about all this men were working, seeing that the mounds of lines led through the right blocks, from the proper place to the proper place; stowing the sails in sail bags and taking the food below.

In this swirl of workers stood Father Armstrong and Father Bredder—Father Armstrong very much at home, leaning against the mizzen shrouds and cocking one eye up the line of the mast; Father Bredder very conscious of being in the way. Sir Harry caught sight of Father Armstrong as he neared the cockpit and shouted, "Hello, Gerry. I'd forgotten you were coming. Been here long?"

"Only a few minutes," said the priest. "I'd like you to meet my friend, Father Joseph Bredder. Sir Harry Stockton."

"Come below out of all this mess," said Sir Harry. "I'm enormously pleased you are coming with me, Gerry. Got a mixed crew—Yanks, New Zealander, one from South Africa, and a couple of our own. And of course everybody's new to the boat. We'll start sail drills tomorrow and by the time I'm through with it, that foredeck gang will quiver at the very mention of a spinnaker. Four thousand seven hundred square feet in that number one, and I'm determined to carry it until she drives under.

"Some of the young fellows these days haven't really got any beef to them. Oh, they're big enough, all right. But they haven't got any hate in their muscle. And to trim a sail in a hurry, as you know, you've got to hate every man-defying inch of it."

While he was talking—in fact delivering a monologue —Sir Harry led the two priests down a surprising spiral staircase into the main salon of the *Maid*. It proved an apartment of enormous luxury, matching anything Father Bredder had seen ashore. There was not a stock item, from the frosted silver lamp bracket to the specially woven carpet of moss green with at its center a compass card worked into the material in red and black. There were upholstered armchairs, covered in watered satin, a curved couch whose surface must have been a full fifteen feet long, bookcases in white oak with small leaded glass panes against the walls or bulkheads, and before each cluster of chairs a low but ample coffee table also in white oak. A faint hum and a welcome chill in the air indicated that the main salon of the *Fair Maid of Fowey* was air-conditioned.

Sir Harry, clad in blue dungarees and a blue workshirt to match, handed a steward a pair of long-nose pliers which he had taken from his hip pocket and sat down on one of the watered-silk chairs.

"Have a pew," he said, indicating chairs beside him. "You can have anything you want to drink. Just say what you wish."

"Tea," said Father Armstrong.

"Green or black?"

"Lipton," said Father Armstrong.

"And you?"

Father Bredder wasn't very fond of tea. But he didn't want to order coffee.

"He'll take a beer," said Father Armstrong. "Plain old Lucky Lager. Anything else is wasted on him."

"Two things the Yanks don't know how to make," said Sir Harry. "Beer and tea." He ordered a whisky and water for himself.

"What do you think of her?" Sir Harry asked with a little jerk of his glass to indicate the whole yacht.

"Nothing like the *Pendragon*," said Father Armstrong who, a little to Father Bredder's surprise, seemed very knowledgeable on boat and sailing matters.

"Different oceans, different ships," said Sir Harry. "The *Pendragon* was excellent offshore in Europe but not the ship for these waters. I had Van Kemper study everything that there was available on Pacific Ocean sailing conditions before starting the design. Weather records, oceanographers' reports, currents, waves—everything. This is what he came up with. You noticed that she had no fin keel?"

"Yes," said Father Armstrong.

"Twin centerboards," said Sir Harry. "As you trim sail above and alter the center of effort, so you can trim the keel below and alter the center of lateral resistance. . . ." He was off in a welter of technicalities whose significance was quite lost on Father Bredder, who had time to look around, marveling that all this elegance was situated in the hull of a yacht. He noted a baby grand piano in one corner of the salon, and was puzzled to find no masts coming through from the deck. There was an elegant wall, covered with mirrors at the far end of the salon, and beyond that he could glimpse another large apartment which he later found to be the dining room. Sleeping quarters were further forward and behind the cockpit he guessed would be the private apartment of Sir Harry—the Great Cabin of this tremendous craft.

He picked up the conversation again at the point where Father Armstrong announced that he would not be sailing on the *Fair Maid* in the Transpac.

"But your father assured me that I could count on you," said Sir Harry. "And I am counting on you, hang it."

"I'm sorry," said Father Armstrong. "But I had the summer planned."

"Confounded nuisance," said Sir Harry. "I must—" He was interrupted by a scream which rose to terrifying proportions and was ended by a thump on the deck above. For a moment there was an appalling silence and then there was a rush of feet on the deck converging on what would appear to be the area at the bottom of the mainmast. Sir Harry was out of the salon in a moment, flying up the circular staircase with Father Bredder behind him. A surprising number of people had gathered in that short while at the foot of the mainmast, but they made way for Sir Harry to pass through.

On the deck in the debris of the bosun's chair lay the crumpled body of a man. He lay on his back, with one leg under him and the other stretched out straight. There was a stream of blood coming from his nostrils and a trickle also from his ears.

"He fell from the top," said the big head rigger.

Father Bredder bent down over the man and knew immediately that he was dead. And Sir Harry said with feeling, "Good God. That could have been me."

Three

"I HEARD you are a friend of Sir Harry Stockton's," said Lieutenant Minardi, looking about his desk with some distraction for a cigarette. He moved a volume of the California Code concerned with Search and Seizure and found a crushed pack of filters between this and a thick file containing pale blue papers. He pulled out a cigarette, broke off the filter tip, and lit the cigarette, inhaling with zest.

"Aren't you afraid of lung cancer?" asked Father Bredder, not for the first time, for his friend's addiction to unfiltered cigarettes distressed him.

"I never give it a thought," said Minardi. "If I did, I probably would be. If you think of anything deeply and in isolation—separated from the rest of living—it becomes frightening. About this Englishman—Stockton—is he a friend of yours?"

"Not at all," said Father Bredder. "Father Armstrong knows him well. If I'd known you wanted to talk about Sir Harry Stockton, I could have brought Father Armstrong along. He'd like to come here, too."

"Why?" asked Minardi.

"He's English," said Father Bredder. "So everything that's American interests him. He's never been in a police headquarters like this."

"Bring him along sometime and I'll give him the special tour. What did you think of Stockton?"

The question took Father Bredder by surprise. "I can't say," he said. "I haven't really thought about him at all. I just have a number of impressions. I saw him only that once, when the man fell from the top of the mast."

"What are your impressions of him?" said Minardi. "Give me everything you felt about him."

When Minardi was serious like this, Father Bredder knew that he must be answered accurately and in detail.

"I thought him a forceful and selfish man," he said. "By selfish I mean egotistical—as if the whole world must concentrate on his needs. He seemed not only annoyed but genuinely disappointed when Father Armstrong said he couldn't go with him to Hawaii. Father Armstrong could answer you better here, but I fancy he is one of the few men with whom Sir Harry Stockton has any real closeness. He seemed to distrust people—even the skilled workmen on the boat. But that might be his egotism—thinking himself more skilled than they."

"When the man was killed, what was his immediate reaction? Pity? Horror? What?"

"Fear, I think," said Father Bredder. "He said it might have been him. And it might have been, too," continued the priest. "He was at the top of the mast in the same bosun's chair only a few minutes earlier. That would make any man afraid."

Minardi blew on the end of his cigarette, watching the ash grow bright, his dark eyes moody and sad. He remained a long time examining the end of the cigarette and then said softly, almost as if he were talking to himself, "Do you believe in Jonahs?"

"I don't understand," said the priest.

"Do you believe that there are certain people who carry misfortune with them—people who are followed about the world by a spirit of malevolence which strikes at others around while leaving them undisturbed?"

"No," said Father Bredder. "I do not."

"We believed in such a thing in Sicily in my boyhood," said Minardi, musing. "The belief was related to the belief of the evil eye. On the door of the house in which I lived —in which I was brought up—there was a design painted to avert the evil eye. And on one of the walls of the convent where I went to school there was the same sign. It is a common sign in Sicily, in fact in the Mediterranean. Somerset Maugham, who lived there, had it printed on the covers of his books. Sir Harry Stockton would do well to have it painted about that beautiful yacht of his."

"Good heavens," said Father Bredder. "Why?"

"Misfortune follows Sir Harry," said Minardi. "He is never himself the victim of misfortune, but those around him are." He reached for the file with the blue paper on his desk.

"I actually shouldn't be concerned with this business at all," he said. "When a man falls from the top of a mast and is killed in a shipyard which is in the jurisdiction of the Los Angeles Police Department, it concerns the coroner's office, but shouldn't be a matter for Homicide. Not really. It's just an accident. Like a traffic death. And so it would be treated if it wasn't for Sir Harry Stockton—and his queer reputation as a Jonah, or perhaps the possessor of the evil eye. I prefer Jonah myself."

"There have been other accidents of this nature?" asked Father Bredder.

"This is the fourth death," said Minardi. "All accidents. Nothing whatever to do with Sir Harry. Except that they all occurred in his—neighborhood.

"Death number one was six years ago. A chauffeur in his employ was killed when a car on which he was working fell off a jack in Sir Harry's garage. Accident. The jack seemingly just keeled over and the man's chest was crushed under the differential housing.

"Death number two was two years later—four years ago." He riffled with thin sensitive fingers through the blue pages of the file. "Henry Skoles, gardener," he said. "Age fifty-eight. Killed when a tree which was being cut down fell on him. Actually a heavy limb of the tree crushed his skull. That was on Sir Harry's place at High Wycombe, which is somewhere near London, I think.

"Death number three. Just a year ago. Edna Phillips, housekeeper, died in her sleep. Gas poisoning. It seems that the servants' quarters were fitted with small gas stoves and she left hers on. She was about sixty—sixty-three actually. Death number four you know about. That's an average of one accidental death every eighteen months among people who knew Sir Harry Stockton. You see what I mean by Jonah?"

"No, I don't really," said Father Bredder. "It's just that Sir Harry is the most famous figure all these unfortunate people knew. They must have had many other acquaintances in common and any of them could also be called a Jonah. But Sir Harry, being famous, gets the reputation."

"Americans haven't got the right psychic approach for these things," Minardi said meditatively. "A nation which has achieved fame by making everything practical, material, and workable just isn't allowed to think of other powers. Which of course accounts for the enormous sale of grotesque and weird comics among American children— and you'd be surprised to know how many grownups read them, too. You couldn't sell those comics in Sicily where I come from. There the dimension occupied by evil is so well understood that horror comics and so on would seem completely trite."

"Surely you don't believe in such superstitions as the evil eye and some people being what are called Jonahs?" asked Father Bredder, slightly shocked.

"Yes, I do," said Minardi. "But not in the popularly accepted sense. People called Jonahs, including the prophet himself, are probably overbearing, unpleasant, righteous personalities whom others are only too glad to blame for any misfortune that befalls their companions. The kind of personality fits the impression you have of Sir Harry. But I have to ponder the question of whether the four accidental deaths among his staff were the result of the carelessness of the victims, or the result of the victims' being engaged in particularly dangerous pursuits, or some unknown factor which I will call—because it amuses me to do so—the Jonah psychosis.

"Now the chauffeur had been seven years in Sir Harry's employ and a chauffeur or automobile mechanic for thirty-five years. The man killed by the tree was a general hand employed on Sir Harry's estates and had, in twenty years' service, removed a number of trees as well as handling other heavy work. And the rigger who fell off the mast had been a rigger at the Southland Boat Works for more than twenty years. So we can rule out inexperience and perhaps carelessness. I know all about familiarity breeding contempt, but workmen develop over the years particular habits of carefulness in things like jacking up cars and climbing masts—and turning off gas stoves."

"It only takes one moment of inattention to kill," said Father Bredder.

"Admitted," said Minardi. "And that will explain one death or two deaths in Sir Harry's retinue. But will it explain three deaths or four deaths? And what about five deaths? Is there going to be another?"

"Among people known to Sir Harry Stockton?" asked the priest. "I should think that highly probable. In fact, if I were to think back over the last six or seven years I could, I am sure, find four or five people I knew who died in accidents."

"Father," said Minardi. "That heavy logic of yours will give me a headache. I agree with you. You are quite right. But this matter of Sir Harry and the rigger's death has been put in my hands, together with this file airmailed from England, together with one of those mild but so forceful suggestions from the police over there that an eye be kept on Sir Harry.

"The reason that an eye is to be kept on Sir Harry is because he is enormously wealthy and if he were to die the affairs of half a dozen of the bigger British companies, ranging from chemicals to shipbuilding, would be thrown into considerable disorder. The chief constable of High Wycombe, Buckinghamshire, England, has received not one but five separate anonymous letters warning that Sir Harry will never reach Honolulu on the *Fair Maid*."

Father Bredder was about to say something but Minardi silenced him with a gesture. "I know," he said. "Letters of that nature about famous people going on a venture here or there are common. They come into every police department

22 ·

in the world and get only scant attention. But Redwood feels that there is something that isn't 'normal' about Sir Harry. And you know how Redwood hates anything that isn't normal."

Father Bredder nodded, smiling slightly. Indeed he knew Captain Ernest Redwood, with his love of regularity in all things, his precisely ordered life and his constant appeal for normalcy so that he was called Normal Redwood by everyone in the police department. Practical, unimaginative, and unemotional, Captain Redwood lived in Altadena where he was active in the Chamber of Commerce, served on the City Planning Commission, scrupulously attended the Rotary luncheons on Wednesday, and found in all these things a great relief from the violent world of his professional activities.

"What precisely does Captain Redwood find not normal about Sir Harry?" asked Father Bredder.

"You'd be surprised," said Minardi. "Not that custom-built yacht designed especially to finish first in the race to Honolulu. Not his yearly assault on some unclimbed peak in the Andes or Himalayas or New Zealand. Not his insistence that everything he has about his person, such as pens and combs and cigarette cases and pillboxes, should be of solid gold. No. Captain Redwood finds all that normal in a man of Sir Harry's station and wealth. What he finds extraordinary are the very things that you find ordinary— namely, the four accidental deaths among his help over a period of six years.

"Of course, nobody can figure Redwood. When he turned this case over to me, he said, 'This man has climbed six or seven mountains covered with ice and never lost a member of his party. Yet his chauffeur is killed repairing his

· *23*

car, his maid is killed sleeping in her room, a man is killed cutting down one of his trees, and another man falls off the mast of his boat. That's not normal, Minardi. Not normal at all.' "

"Captain Redwood doesn't think these deaths were accidental then?" asked Father Bredder.

Minardi gave an elaborate shrug. "Captain Redwood thinks that these deaths, accidental or not—are not normal," said Minardi. "You know, sometimes I wonder about Redwood's grasp of English. Of course an accident isn't normal. It is for that reason that accidents are called accidents."

"What caused the man to fall from the masthead?" asked Father Bredder. "I was attending to the man and did not make any inquiries."

"A snap hook, which is a kind of a self-locking hook, failed and the chair in which Riverton the rigger was sitting fell to the deck."

"It was the same snap hook that had lifted Sir Harry just a little while before?" asked the priest.

"Yes," said Minardi. "The snap hook is being examined in our metallurgical department. My guess is that it was fatigued and failed."

"On a brand-new yacht?" asked Father Bredder. "That would hardly be normal, would it?" Minardi stared at him but said nothing.

Four

FATHER GERALD ARMSTRONG seated at a table in the Persian Room of the Beverly Hills Hotel, conscious of the lighthearted babble of leisure and wealth about him, and grateful to have consumed a *sole bonne femme* that had not turned out to be just fried flat fish, was amused to find himself feeling a certain nostalgia for other days. This was so much as life had been twenty years before, when he was a young man of wealth and wide acquaintance with a doctorate in English which he had earned merely for something to do.

"That I should have become a priest was a miracle," he once told Father Bredder. "But miracles, in my experience, happen with subtlety and refinement and also with simplicity. There is nothing sudden and vulgar about them. And so it was with me. A resurrection took place within me and I, who like Lazarus had laid dead in my tomb, came to life."

It was amusing then that in this superbly appointed hotel dining room he should find himself reflecting on the pleasures of what had been his "tomb days." The glory of Cowes week, for instance, with the Solent a continuing flutter of white sails, and innumerable dinners and parties to be attended and all of them gay. And the fun of Le Mans, eating impossible French ham sandwiches which were invariably stale and drinking champagne. And then the London winter with its theaters and late suppers and clubs. He had been sitting in the Savage Club on Adelphi Terrace watching the fog steal, in the lamplight, past the bare branches of the sycamores when he had heard the first faint whisper calling him to resurrection. Somewhere there was a line about that, he reflected. Campion, perhaps? "God's voice, which is like unto the mist, that with no loud shout, silences the world."

". . . hold north until about 140 west to take advantage both of the current and the brisker winds," said Sir Harry. "Hang it, Gerry, you are not even listening to me. What the devil are you daydreaming about now?"

"Resurrection," said the priest.

"Confounded nonsense," snorted Sir Harry. "I told your father not to send you to Oxford. Damned place reeks of divinity. First-class sailor ruined." He signaled the waiter to pour more wine.

"When you entered that place you call a seminary, you were within a twelve-month of representing England in the Olympics in the Star Class, and you know it," continued Sir Harry. "England needed you then, Gerry. I don't know that I can quite forgive you."

"When I entered the seminary," said the priest, "I was within a twelve-month of losing my immortal soul. Not in any dramatic way. Just by sheer neglect. But that's settled now. And the point is that I am enormously grateful for the dinner, that I hate to disappoint you and his lordship, my father, but I will not be on *Fair Maid* when she makes her splendid record-setting dash for Honolulu."

"The mark of your generation, Gerry," said Sir Harry, "is ingratitude. I've always been very fond of you. And I'm

26 ·

hurt." He said this with such sincerity that Father Armstrong dropped his tone of light banter and said, "I'm sorry. But your way and mine do not run together any more, Sir Harry. I am not any longer my own master, but must use my time, like money lent, to the very best advantage. If you knew how deeply I am convinced of this, you would not try to dissuade me."

"Well, we shall just have to get along without you," said Sir Harry gruffly.

"Having turned you down," said the priest, "I have no claim on you for a favor, but I am going to ask for one anyway."

"What is it?" demanded the other.

"I wish you would take Father Bredder with you to Hawaii. I would be enormously grateful."

"You, too?" snapped Sir Harry.

"You mean someone else . . . ?"

"Certainly I mean someone else has asked the same thing. Policeman. Some kind of a foreigner with a Mediterranean name."

"Minardi?" asked Father Armstrong.

"That's it. I suppose he's American, but he look more a southern Italian to me. Asked me outright whether Father Bredder couldn't come along as a sort of watchdog for me. Is that what you had in mind? Because if you think I need watching, I should say the duty, if it's anybody's, should be yours."

"No," said Father Armstrong. "Nothing to do with being a watchdog. It's just that it would be an enormous event in his life; something quite beyond all his hopes. Something he deserves, too. He's a very good man."

"Yes, but the *Fair Maid* isn't a pleasure yacht going

down to Capri. She's a machine, built especially to win this one race—be first to finish, anyway. Does he know anything about sailing?"

"Nothing," said the other. "He's rural American with four years of soldiering thrown in during World War Two. He's got plenty of beef and a good mind, though. I fancy you would find him useful—as useful if not more so than some of your skilled hands."

"Get along pretty well with people?" asked Sir Harry. "That's the number-one quality, as the Yanks say."

"Excellently," said the priest.

"Is he good with his hands—know anything about rigging—splicing wire, and so on?"

"Not a thing," said Father Armstrong cheerfully. "He can't navigate either. At least I don't think he can. And I know he can't cook. Lord, how I know he can't cook." He reflected for a moment on a dinner Father Bredder had prepared once in the absence of Mrs. Winters, composed of hot sauerkraut and cold Spam, thoroughly baptized with an "instant" cheese sauce.

"On the other hand," he added quickly, "nothing frightens him. No hardship will wring a whimper from him. He could be green with seasickness and yet do what is required of him. And there is nothing that he will not do."

"You're not serious," said Sir Harry. "You know perfectly well that you would never take a man like him on *Fair Maid* if you were skipper."

"I'm entirely serious," said Father Armstrong. "And on the contrary, Father Bredder would be the first man I would sign on aboard *Fair Maid* if I were skippering her to Honolulu."

"Knowing that he can't trim a sail, handle a spinnaker

28 ·

pole, steer a course—or anything?" demanded Sir Harry.

"Knowing that," said the other, nodding. "And knowing also that he has something which far exceeds these mere skills."

"What kind of a something?" asked Sir Harry.

Father Armstrong selected one green grape from a cluster in a bowl before him and popped it in his mouth. "Strength," he said. "Strength like a mountain. The sort of mountain that you can't climb."

But it was not to be so easy for Father Bredder to join the crew of the *Fair Maid*. Sir Harry was a man who disliked to take other people's advice, since to do so suggested a degree of dependence on them. In particular he did not want to take the advice—the forceful suggestion of what he called the "foreign policeman," Minardi—to have the priest aboard as a sort of bodyguard. He had with him, as a personal secretary, a grimly efficient man named Sawyer (who was not to be aboard during the race), and he told Sawyer to find out all he could about the priest and report back as soon as possible.

In a matter of a day Sawyer had compiled a remarkable collection of facts about Father Bredder. These facts showed that he had won the Golden Gloves Boxing Tournament in his youth, gone on to become a contender in middleweight professional boxing, joined the United States Marine Corps in 1941 and risen to the rank of sergeant. Had received the Navy Silver Star for bravery under fire, the British Military Cross and the French Croix de Guerre, as well as other decorations and then crazily, unaccountably, entered a seminary and become a priest of the Roman Catholic Church.

He had been given first a very tough parish in downtown

Los Angeles and then been appointed chaplain of the Convent of the Holy Innocents—a switch that made Sir Harry suspect that the Church of Rome was capable of the same kind of snafus that bedeviled every big organization.

While chaplain of the Convent of the Holy Innocents, he had helped to solve, or had solved by himself, several murders and in doing so had been often in peril of his own life. His hobby was gardening, though he sometimes went fishing. He had also become a scuba diver. It surprised Sir Harry that Father Bredder was a Franciscan—a member of the Order of Friars Minor. With that kind of background he was certain he should be a Jesuit, for Sir Harry had an Elizabethan view of Jesuits—cunning fellows who, under the guise of priest, were actually engaged in other activities like overthrowing governments. This priest had been pushed on him by that foreign detective, so perhaps he was not a priest at all but a policeman. Or perhaps he was indeed a priest but also in the employ of the police force. A priest discovered many secrets or received many confidences which would undoubtedly be of interest to the police. Not a decent fellow like Gerry Armstrong, of course, who had gone out of his head and become a priest, perhaps over some disappointment regarding a woman. But this Father Bredder, not having had Gerry's background, might not be above that kind of liaison with the police.

The point was, why should he have such a fellow on board the *Fair Maid?*

Sir Harry, whisky and soda in hand, looked over Sawyer's report again and picked on scuba diving. "Larsen," he shouted. "Larsen. Have the goodness to drop in here a moment." There was a repectful kind of scurrying, and Sven Larsen, sailing master of the *Fair Maid,* slipped down the circular staircase to stand before Sir Harry. He was a small, tough, broken-nosed Norwegian, his lips and eyes pale and his blond hair cut so close to the head that the dull gleam of his scalp could be seen below the bristle.

"Yes, Sir Harry," he said.

"Is there anyone on the crew who is a diver?"

"Moulter the Englishman."

"Anyone else?"

"No." A far better seaman than Sir Harry, he knew immediately what was in the wind.

"We're racing without the propeller, as you ordered, Sir Harry," he said. "But Moulter has had several training sessions putting it on the shaft, so he can do this immediately after we cross the finish line. Then we can go under power to our slip. He has also been studying the drawings of the rudder, so if anything went wrong there, he would know how to repair it outboard. If it can be repaired."

"Is he the only man who can dive?"

"I could, if need be," said Larsen.

"No doubt. But I should think that in an emergency I would need you on deck. I can't attend to everything myself. And Moulter would need an assistant if diving on the hull. You ought to bear these things in mind when selecting a crew—to get as many skills as possible into the selection of each man. Now I'm going to have to take on board a man whom I don't want at all, purely for his skill as a diver."

"Yes, Sir Harry," said Larsen who had been through this kind of browbeating before. "What's his name?"

"Joseph Bredder," said Sir Harry, glancing for the information at the sheet before him. "He's a priest, but I don't think that matters. He's a good diver and has other skills, I suppose. You'll have to teach him to sail and make himself handy."

This disposed of, Sir Harry softened a little. He had offended Larsen, chiding him on crew selection; he must mollify him now.

"Sit down," he said. "Care for a drink?"

"Thank you," said Larsen and ordered tequila from the steward.

"Did you say the new man is a priest?" asked Larsen when their glasses had been filled.

"Yes," said Sir Harry. "But not the kind of man you envisage. He was a boxer and in the American Marines."

"A priest," said Larsen.

"There's something wrong with that?" demanded Sir Harry.

"This is an important race," said Larsen. "In Norway we have known for a long time that any clergyman on board a boat is a Jonah. We have had one man killed already and the boat has not been tried in ocean weather." He downed his tequila like water, his pale eyes fixed, unwinking, on Sir Harry.

Five

THE TRANSPACIFIC RACE started at noon on July 4th, the
starting position being an extension seaward of a line drawn
through Point Fermin, a little to the west of San Pedro
Harbor. For the week preceding the start, Father Bredder
had been relieved of his duties at the Church of the Holy
Innocents—with the convent closed they were of the lightest, in any case—and had lived and worked aboard the *Fair
Maid*. Sir Harry, using the funds made available for Father
Armstrong, had told the priest to get himself a complete
outfit for ocean voyaging. The Englishman, Peter Moulter,
had offered his advice in selecting these articles and had
gone with Father Bredder to the marine stores in San Pedro
to get what was required.

"Towels are enormously important," said Moulter.
"Hand towels."

"What for?" asked the priest.

"To put around your neck, old boy, when you're at the
wheel. Surprising the amount of water that sloshes down
your back without them. Do you smoke?"

"A pipe," said Father Bredder.

"Ah. Well, better get two-piece oilskins then with pockets
in the jacket and big flaps over them. But they're a bit of a
nuisance because the hem of the jacket catches on things."

"I don't have to smoke," said the priest.

"This trip will be foul enough without depriving oneself of little comforts," said Moulter. Although a grown man, he had the round smoothish face of a child, pink and innocent, the youthfulness of his appearance enhanced by his black and soft hair, which he grew somewhat long. He was actually twenty-six years of age and had, the priest discovered, no regular employment—nor desired any. He made what money he needed selling cars, or boats, or skippering boats or crewing on them. He went freely from country to country, observing and enjoying life and avoiding any permanent responsibility. He was cheerful and plucky and held himself a little apart from the rest of the crew—a shipmate and yet at the same time an observer. He demonstrated his talent for observation by giving Father Bredder a brief sketch of his shipmates during the shopping tour.

"Larsen," he said, "is the best seaman on board. He's better than Sir Harry, who's pretty good himself. He's a bit acid—sarcastic, you know—but otherwise he's undemonstrative. At the end of this voyage, you'll know as little about him as you do now. And that's a pretty secret life, for you will never be more than seventy feet from him for ten days or more. I would like to think that Larsen had a mother, for that would make him human, but I am unable to imagine a Mother Larsen.

"Storey is a New Zealander. Competent. Easy-going. Never criticizes. A good shipmate. Then there's Smith— George Smith. Never knew a Smith called George before. He's a South African and a first-class heavy weather sailor. Rougher it gets, the more he likes it. In light airs, he gets sulky. He doesn't like criticism. I fancy there's a lot of German in him. They can't stand criticism, you know."

"And the British?" asked Father Bredder with a smile.

"You mean the English," said Moulter. "No one criticizes the English any more. It's a pity because that is a sign of our waning importance. My father tells me that in his day to be an Englishman was to be criticized. He loved it."

"Is he a lord?" asked the priest, perhaps a little under the influence of Father Armstrong and Sir Harry.

"Heavens no," said Moulter. "Agricultural laborer. I got my Oxford accent by careful imitation. If I spoke like my father, I'd be cooking aboard. Shaw was right in *Pygmalion*. But on with the parade. After Smith comes Bill Todd, from Australia, Jimmy Woods, a Yank, and Teddy Yamashito."

"From Japan?" asked Father Bredder.

"From Hawaii," said Moulter. "He's the top spinnaker hand."

"That all?" asked Father Bredder.

"There's Francis, the steward, and Ben. Ship's cook," said Moulter. "Don't know their last names."

"You have sailed with most of these men before?" asked the priest.

"Larsen, Storey, Smith and Yamashito," said Moulter. "The rest I've been with only since I got here in April. We've had a few trial races together. You can learn a lot about a man in a couple of night watches."

There were others aboard, too—Fredericks, an older man who was also American and filled the post of navigator and radio operator. And then there was another man who answered to the name of Clancy and who took care of the various engines on board. There were a number of engines, to Father Bredder's surprise. There was a gasoline engine that ran the main generator which supplied the ship's batteries with current. There was a larger generator which took care of the refrigerated compartment in which perishables were kept. There was a large diesel engine which, once the propeller was put back on the shaft, would drive the *Fair Maid* through the water when she could not be sailed. And up forward there was an electric motor which powered the winches which raised the yacht's anchors.

Every man had his own bunk on board, a drawer and a cupboard in which to stow his clothing. Father Bredder had been warned to bring no suitcases—everything he needed was to be brought in a duffle bag. He laid in a stock of the dark and cheap Carolina tobacco which he smoked, and plenty of wooden matches, and promised Barbara Minardi to send her a lei made of seashells from Hawaii.

The day before the start of the race, Minardi took him out to dinner again. Minardi was very thoughtful and for a long time scarcely spoke. Then he said, "I have something to tell you, but I don't want you to make too much of it—or too little either. That snap hook that failed and killed the rigger, the metallurgical people say someone had either been repairing it—or tampering with it. There's a pin which does the work of a latch or bolt in these things. It is spring-loaded and snaps into place, thus closing the hook and giving it its name. Well, the spring was broken. A piece of it had been removed and another piece left. In short, it didn't work. So the hook fell open and the rigger was killed."

"And Sir Harry had been up the mast on the same snap hook only a few moments before," said Father Bredder.

"Yes," said Minardi. "I don't know what to make of it. Suppose the snap hook was deliberately made unsafe. What would be the purpose? To kill Sir Harry? But that is too random—too uncontrollable. Anybody could be killed—someone else in fact was. And Sir Harry was warned. The alternative is that someone tried to fix the snap hook, maybe thought he had fixed it, and then, after the accident, shut up about it. Maybe that's what happened. But I don't like that much either."

"Why?" asked Father Bredder.

"Because these yachting people—particularly the ocean racing set—pride themselves on extreme carefulness in everything they do. And to leave a faulty snap hook on a line intended to raise very important sails is just too amateurish. Anyway, it's something I wanted you to know. The snap hook had been tampered with. So keep your eyes skinned."

"You're anxious about Sir Harry, aren't you?" asked Father Bredder.

"Yes. That's why I got you on board. To relieve my mind. Redwood's giving me the needle. I keep telling him I'm not supposed to even go to work until someone has been done in. He seems to think that in Sir Harry's case I'm supposed to apprehend the culprit before there's a culprit. But I do feel uneasy about him."

"Why?" asked the priest.

"Too much money concentrated in one man," said Minardi. "Too much power. Too much influence. Also because I was born in Sicily."

"I'll watch him," said Father Bredder. "And tell Barbara I won't forget about the lei."

Minardi took out his wallet and gave the priest a twenty-dollar bill. "It'll cost all of that," he said, "and I know you haven't got the money."

"That wouldn't be fair," said the priest, handing the note

back. "Barbara is relying on me getting it myself. It's a sort of little test she likes to set me. Like in fairy tales. She says if everything else fails, I can always pray."

"Does that work?" asked Minardi.

"Of course," said Father Bredder. "But then, up to the present in these kinds of tests, I've never had to." He paused and added, "Perhaps trying is in itself praying."

In the forenoon of July 4th, then, the *Fair Maid* headed under sail for the starting line off Point Fermin. She was so big that she was like a swan among sea gulls upon the water. The wind was light and out of the southwest so that from the harbor to the starting area the big ketch was close-hauled, her sails trimmed in hard on the winches, the mainsail and Genoa describing two lovely slow curves, one perfectly complementing the other.

She heeled just a little in the easy wind and, with no sea running, slipped with peace through the green water. Sir Harry was at the big aluminum destroyer-type wheel, immaculately groomed and very much the master of his ship. Larsen, the sailing master, sat to leeward of him, in the cockpit, eyeing the slot between the Genoa and the main which Father Bredder had by now discovered was the key to speed. Perfectly formed, that slot produced the maximum speed of which the yacht was capable. Allowed to stray from perfection, the slot becoming too wide or too narrow, the yacht immediately lost speed.

Larsen then watched the slot and the Englishman Moulter and the South African, George Smith, handled the Genoa sheets by which the big jib was trimmed with the aid of a winch. Up in the bow Yamashito called out when the set of the Genoa was imperfect along the stay, and the others kept an eye open for other yachts and an ear open for orders.

Fredericks, the navigator, carried a stopwatch and binoculars and was watching the signal halyards on the committee boat. He had stationed himself near a secondary compass mounted on the cabin roof in the forward part of the cockpit and from this could take bearings of either end of the starting line. Of all aboard he was the least tense. Father Bredder had been detailed to help Smith and Moulter with the Genoa sheets if more beef was needed. He did not have to understand what he was doing beyond heaving on a line until told to stop and was grateful for this, for he had never dreamed that the handling of a sailing vessel, even a racing yacht, was so complicated.

All about was a swarm of yachts, some on the same course as the *Fair Maid,* others on the directly opposite course, some intent on crossing her bow, some slipping under her stern—a complicated ballet of yachts, seemingly as light as down on the water, but the least of them weighing twelve tons. A signal gun was fired and Moulter, sittting ahead of Father Bredder, said, "Half an hour to go. Nothing to get shirty about yet."

"Genoa's luffing," shouted Yamashito from up forward. Both Sir Harry and Fredericks glanced at their compasses.

"Wind shifted half a point to the west," said Fredericks, having verified that it was the wind and not the boat that had altered course.

"Time?" asked the Englishman.

"Eleven-thirty, sir."

Sir Harry moved the wheel to pull the ketch's head off the wind and said, "According to the weather report the westerly is supposed to come shortly after noon. It appears that it was not listening. Stand by to tack."

· 39

There was a swift movement of men on the foredeck and in the cockpit—prescise and efficient. Yamashito up forward, lying on his back by the forestay watching the curve of the Genoa, didn't have to be told that the boat was going to change course. He glanced ahead and then to the left, following the curve through the water which the boat would describe as she came up into the wind and then fell off with the wind on her other side, and saw no dangers.

"Hard up," said Sir Harry and, having glanced astern and to windward of him for a second, put the big wheel over. The ketch came up into the wind's eye, her snowy sails were loose for a moment; a soft tremble ran through her mainsail and Larsen said quietly but with firmness, "Let the Genny back. Now. Trim her to leeward." These orders were lost on Father Bredder. He found himself sitting alone on his side of the cockpit, Smith and Moulter having moved across where they were trimming the Genoa in on the other side. The mainsail and the mizzen came over without being touched. Larsen swore softly, his eyes on a dial in the bulwark of the cockpit. "We lost too much way," he said. "Nine knots and then down to four and look now . . . only six and a half. You bastards move like a bunch of pensioners."

"Doesn't do to back the Genoa," said Sir Harry. "Brings her head around a little faster, but stops her in the water." Except for glancing astern at the swirl made by the ship's wake in changing course, Larsen made no comment on this. He fixed his cold eyes on Father Bredder.

"You," he said. "Find out what you have to do and then do it. The time to find out how to trim a sail is before you have to trim it. Yamashito!"

"Yes."

"Get the number one jib and forestaysail ready."

"Number one jib and forestaysail," said Yamashito.

"I said nothing about a sail change," said Sir Harry.

Larsen did not reply. He was wearing (a complete incongruity on board) a felt trilby hat of the type affected by James Cagney in the 1930s. He pushed it back on his head and looked up at the sky, which was quite clear except for a few wisps of cloud spread out like a fan, their focus being in the west. He watched a sea gull soaring high above them, little more than a dark dot in the sky, and glanced from it to the navigator's compass.

"Wind will be about 280 True at the start," he said. "Right in our eyes. Maybe about eight knots and steady. That sea gull's getting it already, but it hasn't reached down here yet. Only way to cross the line will be on the starboard tack."

"I'll make those decisions," said Sir Harry. "Time?"

"Eleven-forty."

He looked about and caught a glimpse of another large yacht behind him. "Who is it?" he asked.

"*Mistral.* Bennington at her wheel," said Fredericks, whose job it was to answer such questions. "To windward of her and about even with her is *Gesture.* Both on the same tack as ourselves. *Gesture* is using double headsails."

"Have Yamashito and the foredeck crew rig the forestaysail stay," said Sir Harry to Larsen. "I will take her up to the line, jibe and when I am running downwind I want the Genoa taken off her and the number one jib and forestaysail rigged."

Larsen gave a thin, satisfied smile, for this is what he had planned himself. "Yes, Sir Harry," he said. "I'll go forward and tell Yamashito to keep those sail bags out of sight until

· *41*

the last moment. No sense tipping off *Mistral* to what we are going to do."

Father Bredder was quite bewildered by these orders and by what took place in the next few minutes. It seemed to him that the world, in a whirl of activity, suddenly spun around through one hundred and eight degrees. One minute the yacht was headed for the imposing bow of *Eventide,* the Committee Boat. The next minute *Eventide* was astern and *Fair Maid* was slipping between two enormous yachts which he discovered were *Gesture* and *Mistral* and which, but seconds before, had been behind *Fair Maid.* Also the yacht was no longer leaning to one side, but upright, and the wind seemed to have died entirely, though the tremendous mainsail was stretched far out over the water. He stole a glance over the side and found that the seeming slow pace of the yacht was a deception. Along her sleek side the water streamed away in dark writhing eddies. Up forward there was a bustling of men. The mountainous Genoa slipped down to the deck and in a trice, another and smaller sail was raised in its place. Then a second sail went up, inside the first and closer to the mast.

"Fifty seconds," said Larsen. "I should have hired my hands in the home for broken seamen."

"White cone's up," said Fredericks. "Ten minutes to the start."

"Wind speed?" asked Sir Harry.

"Eight knots, 165 True."

"Distance to line?"

"Nine hundred yards. *Gesture* and *Mistral* are tacking for the line," said Fredericks. He clapped his binoculars to his eyes and trained them on *Eventide.*

"Blue cone," he said. "Five minutes."

"Tell me when I have four minutes exactly," said Sir Harry.

"Starboard tack. Stand by sheets," said Larsen.

There was a tight silence, interrupted only by the lonely slapping of the water against the ship's side. They were away from the other yachts now, all of which were crowding toward the starting line.

"Four minutes," said Fredericks.

"Hard a-weather," said Sir Harry, and swung the wheel around. *Fair Maid* swerved like a circus pony, held, caught the wind on her port bow and as swift as a lance sped for the starting line. With every sail drawing perfectly, she covered the one thousand yards in exactly five minutes. She went over the line just as the red cone dropped perhaps half a length ahead of *Gesture* and with the empty ocean ahead.

"Bloody marvelous," said Peter Moulter, his boyish face white with excitement. "Bit of a bastard but a bloody marvelous helmsman." If Sir Harry, still seated at the wheel, heard, he gave no sign. Instead, his eyes fixed on the luff of the mainsail, he said to Larsen, "Serve one drink to all hands in celebration of a good start. Then have the liquor locker locked and give me the key. Your next drink, gentlemen, will be in Honolulu."

Six

THREE DAYS LATER *Fair Maid* was alone on the ocean, having pulled away from her rivals and slipped, in the lightest of westerlies, some four hundred and fifty miles north and west of San Pedro. Life aboard for Father Bredder had begun to assume some regularity, though the splendid novelty of his situation still thrilled him. He found it hard to realize that but two weeks ago he had been firmly ashore, concerned over the fruiting of oranges. Surrounded now by the vastness of the ocean and the infinity of the sky, with about him ropes of dacron which were called lines, and winches and sails, life jackets and all the appurtenances of an ocean-racing yacht, it was hard to visualize an orange tree.

"This must be rather like being in heaven," he reflected. "Memories of earth, if there are any, would appear totally unreal. For man, the present is reality, the past and the future become dreams. An orange tree and the ocean . . ."

The incongruity of the thought pleased him, demonstrating the infinity of the mind of the Creator, who on so small a planet as Earth had placed two such dissimilar entities. It was ten in the morning of the third day out and he was off duty. The crew were divided into two watches, called port and starboard—the one under the Englishman Moulter and the other under the South African, Smith. Larsen, as sailing master, and Sir Harry Stockton, as skipper, stood no regular watches, but appeared on the deck at any time. They did, however, spell the helmsman during the day and sometimes at night. The port watch consisted then of Moulter, Storey the New Zealander, Jimmy Woods an American, and Father Bredder. The starboard watch had Smith, Yamashito, Clancy and Bill Todd, an Australian who joined the ship at the same time as Father Bredder but had sailed with Sir Harry before.

The wind was now of the lightest and the sea an unruffled azure which lifted and fell to the rhythm of a slow swell from the north. Smith was at the wheel, irritated by three days of light wind which at the moment scarcely gave the big ketch two knots through the water. The thought that others, *Gesture,* for instance, or *Mistral,* the first somewhat to the north of them and the second to the south, might be getting more air, irritated everybody on board.

"No-good lousy wind," said Smith, watching a dark fold appear in the mainsail. He put the wheel over savagely, bringing a frown from Larsen, who had taken up his usual stand by the mizzen shrouds.

"Not so heavy with the helm," said Larsen. "You will kill her way."

"She hasn't any way," snapped Smith. Fredericks appeared carrying his sextant in its case. He was extraordinarily careful with the instrument, never taking it out of the case until the moment it was to be used, and putting it back again immediately he had read the angle.

"What does the radio say about wind?" asked Smith.

"We're on the southern edge of a high that the Coast Guard knows nothing about," said Fredericks. "Their prediction is light northerlies veering to northeast in this area about midafternoon." He had seated himself on the low cabin top and now, with great care, took his sextant out of its case. "Everybody has fallen into this hole, if that will console you. *Gesture* and *Mistral* as well," he said.

"It is not the North Pacific high?" asked Moulter.

"No. That's two hundred miles north and five hundred miles west of us," said Fredericks. "Don't fret, children; God will send wind when he wishes. Not so, padre?" There was a suggestion of mockery in the question, for Fredericks, despite a genial appearance, had a habit of mockery of which he was not perhaps conscious. Father Bredder did not reply to the question. Moulter had started calling him padre and now everyone had picked up the name except Larsen. He had an anger toward the priest and called him Bredder. Sir Harry never mentioned his name, and he had hardly, partially because of the watch system, exchanged more than a score of words with him since coming on board.

"You're off course," said Larsen. Smith spun the big wheel, watching the compass. He exuded anger, hating light winds and resenting criticism, too, of his helmsmanship. Larsen turned again to watching the Genoa and then left the shrouds and came over to the wheel.

"I'll take her," he said. "You're steering all over the ocean."

"See if you can hold her steady then," said Smith. "Two fifty," and left the helmsman's seat.

The wind now failed utterly. The big ketch, after gliding under the force of inertia for a little way, slowed to a halt. The sails flapped and with each flap, the big boom on the mainsail tugged at its sheet, sending a perceptible shudder through the hull.

Larsen looked bitterly at Smith. "You see," he snapped. "Talk about the wind and it goes. You should know better." He was completely serious.

Todd, the Australian, wet his big forefinger by putting it in his mouth and held it up in the air. Whatever his findings, he was not satisfied with them, for he repeated the process. "Nothing," he said. "Blooming nothing. Straight up the flaming mast."

Yamashito, small and eager, shaded his eyes and looked up and about at the brilliance of the sky. He studied the slow swell and said, "It should come in from the north."

"Quiet," snapped Larsen. He had risen from the seat behind the wheel and now looked about at the ocean and the sky, tense, as if both listening and watching for the wind. He seemed to be feeling for it with his skin. There was only the slightest swaying of the yacht from wave action. Around the boat the surface of the ocean quickly took on the appearance of smooth blue satin. The yacht's head fell off from the compass course, for she had no steerage, and she started to turn a slow circle in the water. The finger on the wind direction finder spun crazily around the dial, through three hundred and sixty degrees, sometimes clockwise, sometimes anticlockwise, as the indicator at the top of the mast was whipped about by the slight motion of the ship.

Sir Harry Stockton arrived on deck, clad in light blue pajamas and a white silk dressing gown.

"Nothing," said Larsen. "Nothing. The air is dead."

"The air is never dead," said Sir Harry. "Get the half-ounce drifter on her." Down came the Genoa and Yamashito disappeared down the forehatch to pop up again with a ridiculously small sail bag. Out of this, to Father Bredder's astonishment, came acres of light blue sail—an ocean of sail out of a bag no bigger than a pillow case, like some trick performed by a French circus clown. But the sail was of sheer nylon, suitable almost for lingerie.

The head was attached to the spinnaker halyard, a light line was put to one corner for a sheet with which to trim it, and the other corner of the sail was fastened to a fitting in the bow of the deck. Hauled aloft, this sail, off some fairy-tale boat, filled and collapsed time and again in a soft dreamy manner. Even Father Bredder could tell that the slight rocking of the mast and not a real movement of the air was what made it fill. Neither main nor mizzen could be changed for lighter sails, for the rules of the race forbade lightweather canvas being carried to replace these.

Sir Harry, taking over from Larsen, ordered these two sails stowed, and with the blue drifter undulating forward and draping itself at times around the shrouds almost as if caressing them, told the watch to raise a light spinnaker on the mizzenmast.

Then he took down the drifter and replaced it with a spinnaker on the main. He next took down the mizzen spinnaker and replaced it with a light mizzen staysail.

For two hours, during which the sun climbed higher, the heat beat down more and more and the huge yacht turned lazy circles in the ocean, he went through sail change after sail change. And all without effect, for Larsen was right and the wind was dead. It was now time for Father Bredder's watch to take over. Sir Harry went below and was followed by Larsen. As he went down into the cabin, Moulter, the watch captain, asked Larsen if he had any orders concerning sails. Larsen didn't answer.

"You take the wheel, padre," said the Englishman.

"Course should be two hundred and fifty degrees, but you'll have no control. Fool around and see if you can nudge her onto the course. Steers like a car. Turn to the right and the ship turns to the right—when there's a wind. You know about compasses; the lubber line, I mean."

"Yes," said Father Bredder. He had had compass training and plenty of it during the jungle war.

"Good," said Moulter. "We'll clear up all this mess of lines here in case the wind ever returns. And if anybody says 'as idle as a painted ship upon a painted ocean' I'll brain him."

He led the way forward and Father Bredder sat behind the wheel of the *Fair Maid,* master of the vessel and at the same time quite powerless. He tried to get control moving the wheel, but there was no response from the ship. After a little while he just sat with one hand on the wheel, glancing occasionally at the compass and listening to the soft flutter of the light nylon sails as the rocking of the *Fair Maid* filled and emptied them with a movement which was paradoxically also a personification of idleness.

The priest indeed became a little drowsy and began to nod off into a lovely warm blue world which was a mixture of mind and eternity, when he heard voices from Sir Harry's stateroom behind him and these, persisting, roused him. He could not tell what was being said, but only that Sir Harry and Larsen were talking. They were not quarreling, but on the other hand, theirs was not a relaxed discussion, for Sir Harry's tone was imperious and Larsen spoke emphatically and shortly, occasionally cutting into one of the Englishman's sentences. Yet not a word could be distinguished of what was being said, and Father Bredder discovered, to his mortification, that he was both eavesdropping and disappointed at not being able to make out the subject of the argument below.

He also felt guilty at having dozed a little at the wheel. Peter Moulter and the rest of the watch were still tidying up the lines forward and packing the huge spinnaker into its bag, a most delicate operation. A glance at the compass revealed that the ship had been making another one of its slow circles in the ocean eddies and now was headed at three hundred and fifty-five degrees, almost due north. A flutter of cold air touched the priest on the forehead. He spun the wheel away from the tiny breeze, for he had been studying the work of the helmsman enough to know something of handling the wheel. The drifter had been set on the foremast and now it filled in a lonely soaring curve. The yacht came instantly alive, moving on the moment through the water with a patter of wavelets against its slim hull.

"A breeze," cried the Englishman. "Two fifty, padre." He deserted the spinnaker to run back and trim the light sheet on the drifter. Main and mizzen had been lowered, but a mizzen staysail was hanging from the mizzen top and now it also filled in the wind.

It was a very light sail, though not as light as the drifter. The priest brought the boat around to two hundred and fifty degrees on the compass. She steered so readily that he could turn the wheel with his fingertips. The rest of the watch, seeing that all was well with the helmsman, set about the task of trimming sheets exactly to the wind. *Fair Maid* started making a faint mushing sound which, contrasted with the utter silence of the flat calm, had a magical quality.

Larsen came immediately on deck, glanced at the dial of the wind vane and the further dial which indicated velocity and said, "Get the number one spinnaker on the main.

Leave the mizzen staysail, but I want the mainsail and mizzen on her. Right now. Turn out the watch below."

Everybody then came streaming on deck, and Larsen shouted to Moulter, "Are you happy with your helmsman?"

"Doing fine," said Moulter. "Two fifty."

So Father Bredder was left at the wheel concentrating on steering the compass course while the rest of the hands crowded sail on the ketch. He felt the cockpit start to throb under his feet and knew that it was eleven-thirty and Clancy had started the gasoline engine which charged the ship's batteries.

The wind, which had started merely as a movement of air and nothing more than that, became first a zephyr and then a good sailing breeze of twelve knots. *Fair Maid* heeled a little, and as more sail was put aloft, increased her speed. She was soon making ten knots. Sir Harry came on deck and without a word took the wheel from the priest. Larsen said, "We can expect the trades in an hour or so. There's a northeast swell already."

Everybody was all at once in a good humor. Smith was close to smiling. Larsen looked relaxed. Fredericks, who had gone below, reappeared with a report that his last sight put them a little further ahead than he had anticipated. "We are in a west-going current," he said. "About one knot. It's pushing us along." All were pleased with him, as if he had invented the current.

And then the steward came up from the main salon, his face white, and looking wildly around, cried, "There's something the matter with Clancy. He's lying on the floor of the engine room. I think he's dead."

Seven

CLANCY WAS not dead but unconscious. His skin had a slight tinge of blue, most marked about the eyes and cheeks, and Father Bredder, who was the first to reach him, dragged him with the aid of Storey from the engine room, up the spiral staircase and into the cockpit and the open air. There he pulled his shirt collar open, flipped him face down on the cockpit floor, and started to give him artificial respiration.

"Carbon monoxide poisoning," he said. "He's still breathing."

"What happened?" demanded Sir Harry Stockton of the steward, who was still pale-faced and very shaken.

"It was time for lunch, sir," said the steward. "I always serve it at twelve-thirty, as you know, and Clancy turns off the generator so there will be no disturbance from the noise. . . ."

"Yes, yes," said Sir Harry. "I know the orders I have given for serving lunch on my own ship."

"Well, sir," said the steward, "the generator was still running, and I thought that Clancy had forgotten the time. So I opened the door of the engine room which, as you know, is just to the side of the corridor under the cockpit. And there was Clancy, lying unconscious on the floor of the engine room. I thought he was dead. He wasn't moving. The engine was still running, and I came up here. I was very frightened."

"Leak in the exhaust somewhere probably," said Storey. "It wouldn't take long to saturate that engine room with carbon monoxide. Poor devil probably dropped before he knew what was the matter with him."

"Makes you feel drowsy at first, they say," said Moulter. "Probably couldn't make it to the door."

Clancy had by now recovered consciousness and Father Bredder, with the help of the others, put a few of the cockpit cushions under him to make him feel more comfortable.

"I think he's going to be all right now," he said. "But keep an eye on him. I'm going below."

"Feeling sick?" asked Moulter.

"No," said the priest. "I want to look at that engine room. In any case the engine should be turned off."

Sir Harry had surrendered the wheel to Storey, and he said, "I'll come with you. That place may still be full of fumes and dangerous."

Father Bredder looked at Sir Harry as if he were about to say something, but remained quiet. He got down to the engine room, however, ahead of the knight. It was reached from a landing at the bottom of the circular staircase. This landing on one side led to the main salon and on the other to a corridor which, running underneath the cockpit, connected with the great cabin in which Sir Harry had his quarters. A small door in the middle of the corridor (which itself was on one side of the ship) gave access to the engine room. The door had a high threshold to keep floodwater out of the engine room, and the big priest could only just get inside. The lights were still on, for there was no natural lighting in this area, and the generator engine, which was a small unit and placed to one side of the main engine which drove the vessel when under sail, was still running.

The priest glanced at the ammeter of the generator and noted a charge of only six amps. He turned the ignition switch and the harsh vibration of the two-cylinder engine ceased. There were several switches on a panel on one of the walls of the engine room, one of them marked FAN, and he turned this on.

Immediately he heard the sound, half between a hum and a whine, of an electric motor. There were two large ducts in the engine room, one on what would be the ceiling and the other in the floor and at the lowest point. He reached up and put his hand over the one at the ceiling and felt cool air coming in. He was down on his hands and knees feeling for suction at the lower vent when Sir Harry joined him.

"That system is to prevent explosions," Sir Harry said. "The fan blows fresh air into the compartment and exhausts any foul air which may have petrol fumes in it. As you probably know, a tablespoonful of petrol, if evaporated into the atmosphere in a closed space, can cause as much of an explosion as a stick of dynamite."

Father Bredder nodded. "Pity Clancy didn't leave that blower on," he said. "It would have taken care of the carbon monoxide." He glanced at the switchboard, "I see you have a secondary ventilator system," he added, nodding to the board.

"Yes," said Sir Harry. "Actually that switch there marked 'ventilator' merely opens a duct to one of the ventilators on the main deck and permits air to be blown down here by the wind. There's no fan."

"And, of course, there being no wind, no air would have

been blown down here," said the priest. He noted that the appropriate switch was in the position marked "on."

"Exactly," said Sir Harry. "We are fortunate that it was not a great deal worse. If Francis had not found Clancy, he might have died. As it is, I expect he will be all right in a day or two. By the way—do you know anything about engines?"

"Enough to start them and turn them off and fill them with fuel when needed," said Father Bredder, which was not strictly true, for he was a good practical mechanic.

"Perhaps you will take over Clancy's duties until he is back on his feet again," said Sir Harry. "All you will have to do will be run this generator once a day for an hour or so until the batteries are charged. And keep an eye on the air-conditioning and refrigerating units."

"I'll be glad to," said the priest.

Sir Harry left then, but lingered in the small door, as if expecting the priest to follow him immediately. "Coming?" he asked eventually.

"No," said Father Bredder. "I want to find out where the carbon monoxide came from."

"Of course," said Sir Harry. "Of course," and went off, leaving the priest to his new work.

Built into one of the bulkheads of the engine room was a gleaming tool chest of ten drawers, and Father Bredder, selecting a few hand wrenches from the top drawer, started checking over the exhaust system of the generator engine. He found a loose flange, and uncoupled the flange to inspect the gasket, which proved intact.

Father Bredder was very fond of engines. He saw in them the handiwork of men, built with care and concern and retaining even in the poorest of them some of the personality of their builders. For this reason he could not abuse an engine and disliked to see one abused. And he noted, as he tightened the second of the two bolts that coupled the exhaust flange, that the head of one of them was a little burred. Two of the corners of the hexagonal head were damaged, so it appeared that someone had tightened this particular bolt before and with an improper tool which had slipped. A crescent wrench had perhaps been used—or maybe a pair of pliers. But only an inferior mechanic would use such a tool on the head of a bolt.

Interested, he examined the head of the bolt with greater care, and then, leaving the engine room, sought Fredericks. The navigator was seated in the room forward of the main salon in which he did his work. It was a cozy little den and Fredericks, who was not without a sense of humor, had put a notice on the door reading: "Interruptions can be disastrous."

Nevertheless Father Bredder knocked on the door and was answered by a grunt of "Come in if you must." He entered to find Fredericks leaning back in his chair, reading a book and at the same time eating his lunch, which consisted of sandwiches.

"Oh, it's you," he said. "I thought it was Sir Harry inquiring about our position again. It's been an hour since I told him, so he must be getting anxious once more. Do you know who loses yacht races?"

"No," said the priest.

"The navigator. Always the navigator. The so-and-so gave a false position so that the ship missed picking up the trades—or the westbound current—or the what have you, and so lost the ship her chance of winning. And you know who wins races?"

"The skipper?" asked Father Bredder, smiling.

"You have the makings of a first-class navigator," said Fredericks. "You have already mastered the most important lesson concerning navigation. What can I do for you?"

"Can you lend me a magnifying glass for a moment? I think I saw you using one the other day."

"But detectives don't use magnifying glasses any more," said Fredericks with a return to his habitual mockery. "That went out with Holmes." Then he said, "Something odd about Clancy?"

"Oh, no," said Father Bredder. "Just curiosity on my part. Why?"

Fredericks shrugged. "One man killed," he said. "Makes you wonder who's next."

Father Bredder made no comment and Fredericks handed him an oblong magnifying glass. "Bring this back, for without it we are lost. I can't read the columns of figures in the 214 Tables."

On his way to the engine room Father Bredder found Francis serving a delayed lunch in the ship's dining room. His own watch, the port watch, consisting of Moulter, Storey, and Woods the American, were seated at the table and they called to him to join them. The priest hesitated and then said, "I'll be with you in a minute. I want to use this and get it back to Fredericks before it gets broken."

"Magnifying glass," said Moulter. "How jolly. Hey, you don't suspect that someone was trying to do old Clancy in?"

"No," said the priest. "I just want to look at a bolt and the light is bad in the engine room." He was a little flustered and did not like his explanation. It raised rather than allayed suspicion. He was only a few minutes examining the bolt and then returned, gave the magnifying glass to Fredericks, and seated himself at the table.

It was part of the pride of *Fair Maid* that menus for all meals were printed on a tiny printing press and choices offered on some of the courses. Father Bredder examined the menu and settled on vichyssoise and assorted cold cuts and potato salad, for though the dining room was air-conditioned, the heat of the engine room had robbed him of his appetite.

"What was the magnifying glass for really?" asked Storey as the priest started on the soup. "Fingerprints?"

"No," said the priest. "I found a bolt with some burring on the head. That sort of thing interests me. I just wanted to look at it more closely."

"It was an accident," said Storey. "Just a silly accident. Like that rigger falling from the mast." The priest glanced at the New Zealander, for the manner in which he mentioned the rigger suggested that he did not really believe that it was an accident. "What's this bolt you were looking at?" Storey asked.

"Just a bolt," said the priest.

"What makes it so interesting then?" Storey persisted.

"Nothing at all," said Father Bredder. "Just an example of what everybody knows and only mechanics believe—namely, that you should never tighten a bolt with a crescent wrench or a pair of pliers. At best you will burr the edges and at worse you will both burr the edges and not get the bolt tight. Whoever installed the exhaust on the generator engine tightened one of the bolts in a flange with a crescent. The crescent slipped and burred the edges of the bolt. Furthermore, the bolt was not completely tightened. So there was a leak in the exhaust. And so Clancy was nearly killed."

"Absolutely fascinating," said Moulter with an enthusiasm which was quite real. "You know, it's marvelous, when you come to think of it, how life can hang on such a little thing as that—an improperly tightened bolt, and the penalty may well be obliteration."

"Not obliteration," said Father Bredder. "Only death. And in any case Clancy was found in time. He has to thank you for that"—turning to Francis, who had just brought him his cold cuts. "He's very lucky that you went to see why the engine wasn't turned off. I suppose you could hear it in the galley?"

"Not so much hear it as feel it, sir," said Francis. "It sets up a little vibration that makes things rattle. And it isn't me he has to thank but Sir Harry. Sir Harry gave the orders that all engines are to be turned off during meals—except the air-conditioning units, which don't make much noise because they're electric. He is very sensitive to engine noise."

"Where's Clancy now?" asked Father Bredder.

"In his bunk forward, resting."

"Anybody taking care of him?"

"I'm looking in on him when I have a chance," said Francis. "Some of us feel that we ought to call that Coast Guard cutter that's accompanying the race and have him taken off or at least examined by a doctor. But it's up to Sir Harry to give the orders."

"I expect he will when he thinks fit," said Moulter a little sharply, as if reprimanding the steward for talking out of turn.

"He won't," said the American, Todd, making his first

contribution to the conversation. "Clancy's all right. And the skipper doesn't want to give away our position. He's not answering roll call. We know where *Gesture* and *Mistral* and the rest of them are. But they don't know where we are. And if Sir Harry has his way, they're not going to find out."

He handed his empty plate to the steward, pushed back his chair and, rising, said, "We're all alone on this junket. Absolutely alone. And that's the way it's going to be until we get to Honolulu."

In the utter silence of the dining room, it seemed to Father Bredder that these words had a somewhat sinister undertone.

Eight

THE WIND which had come up while Father Bredder was at the wheel had now established itself from the north and blew briskly. It had a touch of cold to it, a slight nip which after the lassitude and heat of the calm was very welcome. After lunch, it being a time of leisure for Father Bredder, he went on deck and seated himself forward near the main shrouds, where he had a splendid view of the sea to leeward, all blue and white, where the slim hull of the boat sped through it. A swirling lacy foam extended from bow to stern on the leeward side.

Fair Maid was moving away fast—her wake a boiling pathway astern which seemed for a hundred feet or more to flatten out the ocean itself. The noises of the ship and the wind were quick with energy—a slight sibilance around the shrouds and a splashing and hiss under her leeward rail.

This was all that Father Bredder had ever dreamed of about voyaging at sea—sun and wind and a fine vessel slicing through the water. He looked upward at the graceful shapes of the sails overhead—the colorful spinnaker, banded in red, white and blue; the mainsail, white but touched with purple shadows and shades of pale gold; the mizzen staysail, banded like the spinnaker and aft the mizzen, a duplicate on a smaller scale of the powerful mainsail. All were drawing without a tremor. The masts seemed to lean a little forward and to the side, and the head of the enormous mainmast performed a graceful arc against the lovely sky. It was all satisfying for the priest—good with the kind of goodness God had intended for man. And ahead was a tropical island which, although utterly denuded now of its original population, still had palm trees upon it and a girdle of coral about its lush green hills and mountains. Father Bredder, having lit his pipe and got it going to his satisfaction, decided that he did not really deserve the happiness which he now experienced.

Smith was at the wheel and although Smith hated light airs, he loved this kind of wind. His heavy dark features appeared good-humored and Larsen, leaning against the cabin top where he could eye the main and the dual clews of the spinnaker, seemed also well pleased with life. Even the cook, the man called Ben whom Father Bredder had scarcely more than glimpsed (for he kept close to his galley), came up the forward hatch and, as if not quite trusting himself to the exterior world, remained peering about, with half his torso only above the level of the deck.

He was a small man, with fair hair, which was very sparse at the sides and nonexistent on top of his head. His eyes were gray and had a sort of blind look, and his skin, though white with good red cheeks, had a look to it as if the flesh beneath was a little shrunken. He could be a well-preserved seventy or a somewhat dissipated thirty. He was plump, but plump with a suggestion of wasting, as an apple wrinkled in its skin when overripe. His profession was that of sea cook, a rarity in the world. He would not cook ashore, nor live ashore if he could help it, and had, so Moulter had told the priest, earned his living by cooking at sea all his life.

He turned about to view the full extent of the ship and, seeing Father Bredder, perhaps ten feet away, gave him a little half-hearted wave—a wave which was at one and the same time a gesture of friendliness and also of deference. It was surprising how much the cook got into the wave, and Father Bredder, interested in this somewhat submerged personality of the ship's company, went over to him.

"Nice breeze," he said.

"Yes, indeed, sir," said Ben, putting away a pair of nail clippers he had been using. "Might have a touch of east in it by this evening. If you don't mind my saying so."

Father Bredder did not see that any possible offense could be contained in the suggestion. To put the man more at his ease, he hurried to confess his whole ignorance of ships and weather. This reassured Ben a little, though not so greatly as to make him bold. Still only half emerged from the underdeck, he looked about him carefully, as if to be sure that the liberty he had taken in popping his head up had not been observed, and said, "I fancy we'll be about thirty north right now. Maybe thirty-one, but that would be the limit of it. Of course, I'm no navigator. No. Not at all. Don't know the first thing about it. But thirty-one north would be the limit, I'd say. And maybe one twenty-seven west."

"And how would you know that?" asked the priest.

"Oh, I don't know it," said Ben. "Don't mistake me on that. I don't know it at all. I just guess it, you see. But I'll tell you how I guess it—if you're interested at all."

"I am," said the priest.

"Well," said Ben. "It's the bird there—see it? That one with the long tail that's fluttering so hard and seems to be having such a hard time flying." Father Bredder looked in the direction in which Ben was pointing and made out a creamy white bird, about the size of a pigeon but with a tail at least twice its length and consisting it seemed of one ridiculously long feather.

"Bosun bird that is," said Ben. "Now they don't ever get north of thirty-one. And they don't like to get out of the trade wind area. So the trade wind comes in here around thirty-one north, maybe thirty, but likely thirty-one. And about one twenty-seven west. So looking at that bird, and seeing the wind is brisk and from the north, I'd say that in a couple of hours it will haul to the east and settle into a regular trade."

"You've been at sea a long time," observed the priest.

"I have, sir," said Ben. "Forty-six years come next Christmas. My first day at sea was Christmas. On a lumber schooner out of Seattle. The cook was drunk, do you see. So I offered to cook and that's what I've been doing ever since. And there's people will tell you that there's no good ever came of drunkedness. Why, it gave me the chance of my lifetime."

He was quite serious in saying this, so Father Bredder did not laugh. "You like cooking. Ben?" he asked.

"I do, sir," said Ben. "But at sea. I tried it on land but it's no good. The galleys they have on land are too big. You walk your feet off making three meals. And they're dirty. Never find dirt on a ship like you find on land. But cooking's changed, like everything else. And changed for the worse."

"And why's that?" asked the priest. "I would have thought it had become easier."

"So it has, sir," said Ben. "But because something's easier

don't make it better, if I may say so. It's dull now. Because of all those canned and frozen foods and so on. In the old days you had potatoes and carrots and onions and mostly pickled meat. And flour and dried peas. Something to work with—use your imagination. Now you just open cans or thaw food out. You've never tasted pea soup until you've had it made out of dried peas with salt pork and a touch of thyme thrown in to take the fat taste off the pork. That was my best dish on the old *Henry S.* Two big bowls of that, and three fingers of whisky and I've known men to stand four hours' watch, beating to windward in a sleet storm and never swear once. Did you like that soup you had for lunch, sir?"

"I did indeed," said Father Bredder.

"Well, it was nothing but potato soup but given a fancy French name. But I can make it better with potatoes. That soup came out of a can. I have to serve it. But I'd sooner make it myself."

"And why do you have to serve it out of cans rather than make your own?" asked Father Bredder.

Ben took another look about the deck. "If I told you, you wouldn't believe me," he said.

"I believe most things people tell me," said the priest. "I'd like to hear."

"Well," said Ben. "Potatoes aren't modern. Potatoes is out of date. Canned food is modern, but natural food isn't. Ever been to a supermarket—say in midsummer when there's plenty of vegetables for sale? Ever watch the people buying? Do they buy those fresh garden peas and greens and so on? No, they don't. They buy frozen peas or canned peas." He was very serious as he added, "Everything in the world is getting more and more phony. About all that's left is the air and the sea. And they're lousing up the air something terrible."

He gave Father Bredder a look out of those blank gray eyes which had a subtle cunning to it. "Forgive me asking the question, sir. But is it true that you're a preacher?"

"Yes," said Father Bredder. "I'm a Roman Catholic priest."

"I heard you were a detective shipped to keep an eye on Sir Harry lest he come to any trouble."

"What trouble could he come to?" countered the priest.

"Might cost me my berth if you say a word about it," said Ben.

"Then I won't say a word about it," replied Father Bredder.

"Well, it seems to me that an accident is trying to catch up with Sir Harry. Kind of as if death was chasing him and reaching for him and getting the wrong guy. They do say that death is blind."

"Justice is blind," said the priest.

"No. Justice is stupid. Death is blind," said Ben with finality. "Like that rigger falling from the bosun's chair. Sir Harry had been in that chair not half an hour before. And then Clancy, although of course he didn't die. Still he could have died. And Sir Harry is always going in and out of that engine room, starting the engines and stopping them and tinkering with them."

"He is?" asked Father Bredder, who knew nothing of this.

"Oh yes. You see, Sir Harry don't trust anybody. Everything that's done he has to poke his nose into and see if it's done right. He even comes into the galley to see if I'm cooking things right. And God help me if he finds me boiling soup. That's got to simmer. Never boil. Well. It's been nice talking to you. Don't hold anything I said against me, will you?"

"Certainly not," said the priest.

Ben ducked down below the level of the deck but only to pop up again. "I got a favor to ask you," he said. "No offense."

"Go ahead," said the priest.

"Could you give me a blessing? I don't think I've ever been blessed in all my life."

"Certainly, Ben," said Father Bredder and pronounced the benediction, making at the same time the sign of the cross.

"What do I owe you?" said Ben when it was done.

"Nothing whatever," said Father Bredder. "You know I can't bless you. God blesses you through me. So if you feel you owe anything it would be to God."

"Well," said Ben. "That would take some figuring out, that would," and he popped down the hatch.

Father Bredder had been vaguely conscious since the start of the voyage of a conflict of personalities on board the *Fair Maid*—between Sir Harry and the sailing master Larsen, who was, it would seem, a better sailor. And between Larsen and Smith. Moulter, it was true, was friendly. Fredericks, the navigator, was slightly contemptuous of Sir Harry and Larsen. Todd, the Australian, said very little and Yamashito, the Hawaiian, was concerned only with sailing. But Ben was a treasure. He more than any of the others conveyed a sense of reality and of what was wholesome in life.

Potatoes and bosun birds and a request for a blessing. A career that had started on the chance of a cook on a lumber schooner getting drunk and had been followed for almost half a century with devotion. Yes, Ben was well worth knowing, and perhaps there was more in Ben's life than there had been in Sir Harry's or Larsen's.

And what a fine picture Ben had conjured up of death —death as a blind figure grasping and holding whoever came within reach. No. More than that. Death as a messenger seeking one person but, in its blindness, killing others.

Was death really aboard this ship, blindly groping for Sir Harry Stockton? Father Bredder dismissed the thought immediately as a nonsensical fancy. He glanced back along the slim deck to the cockpit where Sir Harry, Fredericks and Larsen were crowded together examining a chart. Larsen lifted up his head to give a new course to the helmsman. "Two forty," he said, and then, "All hands to trim sail. Get that spinnaker pole up higher."

All hands, Father Bredder realized, included himself, and he went aft to the cockpit to help handle the starboard guy on the main spinnaker. A shoal of silver, like a handful of coins, flung out of the ocean by the side of the ship, veered upwind and fell back into the magnificent blue. Flying fish. The priest had never seen any and he stopped for a moment to watch this traveler's tale coming true.

"You. Get back in the cockpit here," said Larsen. "Move. This is a race, damn it."

Father Bredder, without a word, tailed on cheerfully to the end of the guy, still very pleased about Ben.

Nine

BEFORE HE WENT on watch that particular evening, Father Bredder had a chance to talk with Clancy. He had tried to see him several times, but either there was someone else in the forecastle or Clancy was asleep. However, twenty minutes before the change of the watch he went to the sick man's bunk and found him awake and ready to answer questions.

"How was it that you couldn't get out of the engine room in time?" asked the priest. "Did you pass out before you knew what was happening to you?"

"Something like that. It was like a nightmare where you can't help yourself," said Clancy. "It came on very gently. I began to feel real sleepy and got a bad headache. I figured I needed fresh air and headed for the door, but I couldn't get it open."

"It was stuck?"

"I couldn't turn the handle," said Clancy. "I couldn't think very clearly. Maybe I was trying to turn the handle the wrong way. Anyway, it wouldn't turn. I could feel it turning a little way, but not enough to open the door."

"It's a pity you didn't think to turn on the exhaust fan first," said the priest. "That would have got rid of the fumes and you could have worked on the door at your leisure."

"I did turn it on," said Clancy. "But it didn't work. You can hear the whine of the electric fan when it's working. Even above the noise of the engine. And it didn't work. I snapped the switch off then. That's a habit with me. I never leave the switch on if something doesn't work. There are a lot of accidents from leaving switches engaged on 'dead' engines."

"That's odd," said Father Bredder, "because when I went down, the exhaust fan was working. I tried it myself. And I'm sure I was the first in the engine room after we got you out. I know it was working. I could hear the motor and feel the suction through the vent."

Clancy shrugged. "Electric motors aren't reliable at sea," he said. "Just a little corrosion on terminals from salt air and they short out. Then something happens and they start working again. That whole exhaust system ought to be checked through. Don't ever try to start the engine if that fan doesn't work, though, or you may blow up the whole boat."

"I won't," said Father Bredder. "By the way, did you suspect that there was a leak in the exhaust system? Had you worked on it at all?"

"When I joined the ship in San Pedro, I checked everything on all engines. I didn't especially work on the exhaust on that generator engine—no more than on any of the others. Why?"

"Were there any other workmen in San Pedro tinkering with it?" asked the priest.

"Not to my knowledge," said Clancy. "Oh, yes. That engine was installed in England and had its own outlet through the hull. When the *Fair Maid* was hauled in San Pedro, it was changed to vent through the exhaust of the main engine."

"Why?" asked Father Bredder.

"Cut out one through-hull fitting," said Clancy. The priest looked puzzled. "Cut out one hole through the hull," said Clancy. "The less holes or ports you have through the hull below water, the better off you are—from the point of view of safety and speed. Every fitting that goes through the hull makes a little eddy and slows the boat a bit. Every fitting that goes through the hull below water is a danger spot."

The priest asked Clancy a few more questions about the times he ran the generator each day and for how long. Also, since the duty had now been given to him temporarily, he asked about the working of the air-conditioning unit and the refrigerator. Both were electrically operated from the storage batteries and the principle in both cases was the cooling of air by passing a stream through super-cold gas in a heat exchange arrangement. Water, which condensed out of the air, went into the bilges where, the hull being aluminum, it posed no problem of rot. But it was important, Clancy said, that Father Bredder pump the bilges (by electric pump) each day. The electric pump operated automatically if the bilge water rose above a certain level, but Sir Harry wanted the bilges kept dry and so pumped regularly.

Somewhere, Father Bredder felt, there was a touch of malevolence rather than accident in what had befallen Clancy. But he could not tell where. It was now time for him to go on duty, and he left Clancy for the deck, his mind uneasy, though he could not identify the cause of the unease.

The wind had veered more to the east as Ben had predicted and settled into a full trade wind. It was warm, almost languorous, and was felt on board as but a mild breeze, for *Fair Maid* was making a steady twelve knots and fleeing before the wind its velocity was reduced for those on board. It was odd to see the indicator give a wind speed of seven knots and note that the boat was traveling at twelve knots at the same time.

"Don't touch a sail without my orders," said Sir Harry as he went below following the change of the watch. But he was not below twenty minutes before Larsen ordered main and mizzen brought in a trifle and Father Bredder noted that when this was done, the *Fair Maid* picked up an additional half knot.

Father Bredder, with help from Moulter his watch captain, was learning all he could about sailing. He was becoming much more useful now. He had learned how to belay a line so that it could be undone in a fraction of a second—how to tail on a line and keep a steady strain when a sheet was being winched in; learned never to stand or work with his legs one on each side of a line which was under heavy strain lest it give; learned never to leave winch handles on winches, and so on.

He had also learned the technical terms for the different items of rigging, and Moulter made the discovery that Father Bredder was a natural helmsman. He had a feel for the boat and the wind which Moulter said others never got. This sense of the boat and the wind was especially useful at night, when the sails could not be seen and indeed the whole vessel disappeared except for the misty glow forward of the port and starboard lights and the subdued aura of the binnacle.

At night Father Bredder produced his best work as a

helmsman, sensing immediately an increase in the velocity of the wind, or any falling off in its velocity before the ship itself began to react. He was then allowed to take a spell at the helm with the rest of his watch at night and enjoyed the lovely shape of the sails against the starlight sky and the sense both of sadness and of intimacy which settled over the ship when the night came.

That evening Father Bredder was given the wheel for the first half hour after sunset. The wind was steady, a huge stream of power before which the ship fled west and south, cutting a white and seething line over the sparkling ocean. With the setting of the sun—a sad event at sea, though magnificent on land—a silence, as always, seemed to settle over the ocean and the ship. The crew spoke, it seemed, in gentler tones and the watch on deck moved with softer movements. Storey and Woods had gone forward, half to keep an eye on the spinnaker and spinnaker staysail and half to escape the surveillance of Larsen. Moulter, who was not easily disturbed, had settled down comfortably in the cockpit in such a position that he could keep an eye on the mainsail and give an occasional glance at the compass. Larsen went below and in the night silence Father Bredder got enough privacy to be able to go over all he had learned about the accident to Clancy in an attempt to discover what particular detail of the accident made him uneasy.

There was the matter of the tampering with the exhaust by an unskilled mechanic which had resulted in the burring of a bolt which had not been properly tightened. And out of this had come the leak of carbon monoxide gas which in the limited space of the engine room had nearly proved fatal to Clancy.

Had the bolt been tampered with for a legitimate

purpose—or to produce the carbon monoxide leak? Clancy said the exhaust had been rerouted in San Pedro. But surely a workman in a shipyard would not take a pair of pliers or a crescent wrench to a bolt when he had a whole kit of tools available. There was something wrong about this very aspect.

The exhaust had been installed originally in England, the priest remembered. It seemed to him that there was something significant here. Then he remembered having heard it said that English sizes in nuts and bolts were not the same as American. American nuts might not fit English bolts, and that being so, a workman rerouting the exhaust in San Pedro might use a crescent or even (though this seemed unforgivable in a mechanic) a pair of pliers or channel locks.

So it was possible, after all, that the leaky exhaust had its origin in San Pedro and was unplanned. The priest glanced from the compass to the dark shape of the mainsail, found all well, and went back to his speculation.

What then about the ventilation fan—the electric fan which sucked fumes out of the engine room? Surely it was curious that that had not worked for Clancy? Or was it? Wasn't Clancy's own explanation quite logical—the terminals had become corroded in the damp air, causing a temporary break in the circuit. Flicking the switch off and on was sufficient to restore the circuit. If Clancy had done that himself, all might have been well for him. Perhaps he had done so, but just once more was needed, and that once more had been supplied by Father Bredder himself and not Clancy.

Was there something odd in that switch? Perhaps, examined in isolation, there was something odd in its failure to work. But Father Bredder, letting the wheel slip through his hands for a moment and then catching it, remembered a warning given to him once by Lieutenant Minardi.

"Everything examined in isolation appears odd," Minardi had said. "And it is odd because nothing exists in isolation. Everything is connected to something else. Always look at the whole picture. If there is something odd about that, then investigate. Otherwise you are wasting your time."

Father Bredder realized with a sigh that he was doing just what Minardi had warned him not to do—examine details one by one. The exhaust, the ventilator, the stuck door. They had all to be taken together. Here was a trinity of mischances which had nearly cost Clancy his life. Was there something sinister here? There was always a series of mischances in any fatal accident, he reasoned—a grim piling of step upon step which resulted in death. There was really no reason why he should suspect anything but an accident in Clancy's case. And yet, he sensed something wrong, something spiritually wrong in the accident to Clancy.

What was it then that was spiritually out of tune; what was it that suggested to his mind that here was not mere accident but evil; here was not just a casual hazard to life but a planned threat to life?

He sensed a little change in the wind speed and direction and moved the wheel to compensate. The huge ketch heeled a little when the gust took effect and the dial of the knot meter—a green line moving over small green dots—showed thirteen knots.

"Very nice," said Moulter from the comfortable couch he had made for himself in the cockpit. "Very nice indeed. Now let her come back. But I see I don't really have to tell you. You must have Norse blood in you somewhere. You

· 75

have a nice hand on the helm."

To this Father Bredder made no reply, for he had been reprimanded by Larsen for talking while he was at the wheel and although Larsen wasn't about, he had decided that he would observe that rule of silence.

"I have a theory," said Moulter, "that all winds travel in circles, or perhaps I mean that they travel in arcs. That is to say that the wind does not blow in a straight line but in a curve and this curve may have something to do with the rotation of the earth. If I were not such a lazy dog, I would research this theme and write a very learned piece about it indeed. But I thank God that he made me a lazy dog."

Father Bredder, though he was listening with interest, made no comment.

"Not only do all winds blow in circles," said Moulter, "but I am beginning to think that all lives are lived in circles, and that (barring accident) life is complete when in extreme old age we return to infancy. *Ex nihilo ad nihilum* or something of the sort. Also days are circles and months and years are circles and space is probably a circle. If space is a circle, then eternity is the circle of space transformed into the dimension of time—or perhaps I mean no-time.

"From all this it is plain that the proper symbol of the divinity is not an equilateral triangle representing the trinity, but a circle representing no beginning and no end and . . . well . . . I was about to say no object; that is a circle, or the circumference of a circle, doesn't travel anywhere. But you're at the wheel and so cannot argue back with me."

Again Father Bredder, his eye on the compass, and giving an occasional glance at that enormous and satisfying shadow which he knew to be the mainsail, made no reply.

"Tragedy," continued Moulter, "is an interrupted circle; the destruction of that which is perfect, the prevention of that which is natural. Atheists are men who think a circle is merely a geometrical figure and who do not bother with the fact that neither its circumference nor area can be precisely measured.

"For myself I find it enormously consoling that this is so. How horrible if we had techniques which could resolve every problem, and no lovely unknown whispered darkly to us to venture a little further. Storey! See if you and Woods can drop the inboard end of the spinnaker pole a hair. The spinnaker is not lifting as freely as it should. One moment, I'll give you a hand."

He went forward quickly and quietly as a cat, leaving Father Bredder wondering what it was about his particular class of Englishman that made them all seem as if the world was their toy. Moulter was back in a moment and, ignoring the priest, immediately inspected the knot dial showing the boat's speed.

"Ah," he said, satisfied. "A fraction of a knot. Perhaps it will mean nothing. And yet, in 'sixty-five *Big Ti* beat *Stormvogel* after twenty-five hundred miles of racing by only a few minutes. So it could mean everything. I'll take the wheel now, padre, and you, without addressing a word to the helmsman, which as you know is utterly and properly forbidden, can speculate on the fascinating thoughts I have suggested concerning the circularity of all things."

"Two forty," said the priest, surrendering the wheel and giving the course as he had been instructed to do.

"Two forty it is and all mine," said Moulter. "Except Sir Harry," he added. "He's what you chaps call a square."

"Square?" echoed the priest, for the *non sequitur* was so

abrupt that for a moment he forgot the rule about not talking to the helmsman.

"Not circular," said Moulter. "Not part of the beauty of the circular finite world and the circular infinite universe. Odd, my boy. Very odd, is Sir Harry. A bit of a bastard and as I remarked before, an excellent helmsman." With that the Englishman fell silent and Father Bredder, seated in the now dark cockpit, turned to reflect once more on the problem of what was spiritually wrong with the accident to Clancy.

His thoughts, however, kept getting mixed up with Moulter's circular view of life and all things on earth—a view which the priest found novel and pleasing but which he was sure that Father Armstrong, with his more agile mind, could either expand enormously or destroy utterly, according to which course took his fancy.

He wondered vaguely whether some form of circularity applied to Clancy's accident. Was an accident rather like a circle, going through points equidistant from a center which could be labeled time, place, mischance one, mischance two (or neglect one, neglect two), and on to effect? Perhaps so. Perhaps a perfect accident might be conceived as a perfect circle.

He began to feel a little excitement as if he were approaching some discovery which for the moment evaded his mind. All right, he said to himself. If the series of events which lead to an accident constitute as it were a circle, then anything outside that series of events would bend the circle and the happening would not therefore be an accident. It would be the opposite of an accident. Something that was planned.

In Clancy's case there was a leaking exhaust valve and a

door that would not open and an exhaust fan which had shorted out for the time being. Possibly all three could be said to be mischances which were points along the natural circumference of the circle. There had to be the leaking exhaust, and there had to be the inoperative ventilation fan, and perhaps there had to be the door that would not open. Anything else?

Yes. Of course there was. Something very important. The exterior vent, not a fan, through which fresh air would normally reach the engine room. That had been open. But no air had come in because there was no wind!

That was it. The true circle should consist of the leaking exhaust and the shorted-out fan and the lack of wind; or the exhaust and the lack of wind and the stuck door. But it should not consist of all four—exhaust, lack of wind, shorted fan, and stuck door. That was too much. The stuck door was excessive—a point outside of the natural circumference—a point through which the circle had been bent. It was one point too many.

He stared at Moulter, now seated at the wheel, who with his talk of circles had shown him what was wrong with Clancy's narrow escape from death.

"The course we are sailing," said Moulter, "is a great circle course, which in a circular world is the shortest distance between any two points. And in a little while the circular moon will be up. What a pity indeed that I am such a lazy dog."

Ten

THE FOLLOWING MORNING—that is, the morning after the accident—Sir Harry summoned Father Bredder to his stateroom in what was called the Great Cabin behind the cockpit. There were two entrances to his luxurious apartment—one from a companionway through the deck and just aft of the mizzenmast; the other at the end of the corridor which led under the cockpit, from which corridor the engine room was also entered. Thus, in foul weather, Sir Harry could go from his stateroom to the main salon of *Fair Maid* or any other part of the vessel belowdecks without getting on deck.

The message that Sir Harry wanted to see him was brought by Larsen, who seemed a little pleased at the summons, as if he was enjoying in anticipation what was to take place. When he got to the stateroom, it was to find Sir Harry seated at a lovely desk of rosewood which was built into one of the bulkheads, and writing in a book with a cover of pale blue leather.

"Ah," said the knight, "good of you to come so soon, Bredder. Just a moment, and I'll be with you. Take a pew." He motioned to a miniature armchair, well upholstered and covered with one of those flowered prints with a shiny surface which Father Bredder vaguely identified as chintz.

There were two such chairs in the Great Cabin, plus a small couch and a genuine bed—a miniature four-poster of rosewood. Indeed, the apartment was paneled in the same wood, and had on each side two large portholes which at this time were covered by flowered curtains. The floor was carpeted in dove gray and the whole place was both intimate and luxurious, and seemed more luxurious because it was on a yacht.

Sir Harry scribbled on for a while as Father Bredder took in the details of the apartment, noted the shower with its frosted glass door set in a chrome frame—or could that frame possibly be silver?

"If I don't get this thing written each morning, I find that details escape me," said Sir Harry, indicating the book in which he had been writing and from which he now turned. "Thank you for being patient."

Father Bredder, a little uncomfortable in the undersized armchair, said nothing. He sensed that Sir Harry wanted to say something to him that wasn't pleasant and didn't know how to start, and he sympathized with him.

"How long have you known Gerry?" asked the knight as the best opening he could devise.

"Gerry?" echoed the priest. "Oh. Father Armstrong. About four years now. In fact, four years in November."

"I don't mean any offense," said Sir Harry, "but there was a very fine sailor lost in him. I'm perfectly well aware that the world needs what are called 'men of the cloth,' but it always seems a waste to me when . . ." He sensed that he was headed into murky ground and stopped. Father Bredder grinned.

"When a man with an outstanding talent becomes a priest?" he asked.

"Well, I hadn't quite meant that," said Sir Harry.

"You should talk to my bishop when you return to Los Angeles," said Father Bredder. "He takes the opposite point of view. He thinks it a waste when a man with an outstanding talent doesn't become a priest."

"Oh?" said Sir Harry. "Has your bishop a particular talent himself? I mean outside of . . . er . . . divinity or theology."

"Yes," said Father Bredder. "Real estate. In a dozen years or perhaps a bit more, he has built perhaps a score of schools and a fine university out of ventures in real estate. Some of the biggest real estate men in Southern California go to him for advice."

"Hmmmmmm," said Sir Harry with approval. "Well, this isn't exactly what I asked you to come here to talk about. The fact of the matter is I'm concerned about what happened to Clancy yesterday. The whole thing was an accident, of course—nothing but an accident. But coupled with the unfortunate death of that rigger, I am concerned about the effect on the crew.

"Sailors are strange people, Bredder. Very odd people indeed. Ashore I don't suppose they differ so very much from the rest of humanity. And the point could be made, of course, that the whole of humanity is a trifle odd. But on board, certain characteristics tend to come to the fore. Among them is . . . er . . . well, I suppose I will have to call it an increase in . . . er . . . brooding. What I mean is that anything that happens becomes magnified—is given far too much thought and with far too much effect on the mind. In short, the accident to Clancy, coupled with the death of that rigger, two events which ashore would probably be soon forgotten, is beginning to demoralize my crew a little. There is some kind of talk about this being an un-lucky ship.

"Naturally I don't want that kind of thing at all. What we have to do—what we all have to do—is to de-emphasize the accident to Clancy. Take it as part of the day's work, as it were, and pass it by. And that brings me to you. I'm not saying that you are guilty of anything deliberate or disloyal to me as skipper. Not at all. Not for a moment. But Larsen has pointed out to me that you were making certain in-quiries about the accident to Clancy that rather emphasized it; gave it almost a sinister turn. And while, as I say, I don't for a moment think that you intended such a result, I do want to appeal to you to watch this kind of thing in the future.

"In short, I want you to say nothing further or make any further investigations into the accident. Just let us all forget about it and go ahead with our primary task of winning this race—or rather of being first to cross the line at Honolulu. I am sure that I can rely upon you for your cooperation here."

Father Bredder said nothing for a while, not out of chagrin but out of admiration for the manner in which he, quite innocent, was being turned by Sir Harry into a culprit while at the same time being eloquently assured that this was not the case. He tried to decide how this effect was achieved. It originated in a stance of authority and it was given fuller effect by assumption of reasonableness, of un-derstanding and of righteousness. The bishop had the same ability and used it in dealing with those priests whom he suspected had an eye on headlines rather than on heaven. But Father Bredder had not this talent and perhaps because he lacked it was impressed.

"Well," said Sir Harry, disturbed by the priest's silence, "as I said, I presume that you will give me your full and loyal cooperation in this matter."

"Oh, yes," said Father Bredder, flustered that he had not as yet replied. "Of course. I don't want to upset the crew at all. But they did question me about the magnifying glass and of course I couldn't lie about it."

"Magnifying glass?" asked Sir Harry, and the priest explained. Sir Harry was a little impatient during the explanation and when the priest got to the part about the bolt being of English manufacture and therefore of a different size to American bolts, he brushed that off.

"Pure myth," he said. "The English system is based on inches and feet and was borrowed from England by America. English spanners—you call them wrenches—are made in fractions of an inch and so are English nuts and bolts. Just like American. The only difference lies in the number of threads per inch on a bolt—in short, Whitworth thread versus your American machine thread."

"Really?" asked Father Bredder. "So an American wrench could be found to fit an English nut or bolt."

"Of course," said Sir Harry. "Metric system is only used on the continent."

Father Bredder considered this piece of information, wondering why a mechanic in a reputable shipyard like the Southland Boat Works might have used an improper tool to tighten an exhaust flange. The alternative was that the flange had been tampered with on board, and not at the shipyard.

"Sir Harry," he said. "Do you know where Clancy keeps his hand tools?"

"In those drawers against the bulkhead, of course," said

the knight.

"He has a complete set?"

"Naturally. Everything. I take pride in checking that kind of detail myself."

"Thank you," said Father Bredder, and rose to go.

"I am glad I can count on you," said Sir Harry. "The sooner everybody forgets about the accident, the better for us all."

"It wasn't an accident, Sir Harry," said Father Bredder slowly. "Someone was trying to kill *you,* thinking you might be in the engine room at that time, since you go there quite often."

"Me?" cried Sir Harry. "Have you taken leave of your senses?"

"No," said the priest. "I haven't. But there is someone on board this ship who intends to kill you. The only accident about Clancy was that Clancy was the victim whereas it was intended that you should be the victim. Your primary task, Sir Harry, is not to get to Honolulu first; it is to get to Honolulu at all. I warn you very solemnly never to be alone in your cabin without locking the doors. And whenever you are about the decks, be sure that several people are in plain sight of you. Of course, I won't say a word about that to any of the crew and I'm sure you won't either."

As he closed the door, Father Bredder thought for a moment that perhaps his little address to Sir Harry might have been as effective in its way as Sir Harry's had been to him. And then he realized that this wasn't so. He hadn't Sir Harry's style or authority. But he hoped that Sir Harry took solemn notice of what he had said.

Eleven

BY MID-RACE, lack of sleep from constant sail changes, often made at night, began to tell on the crew of *Fair Maid* and their faces were no longer tanned and rested but tanned and tired; the lids of their eyes were a little red, their tempers a trifle short.

To give the *Fair Maid* an advantage over her two principal rivals, Ted Wirth's big ketch *Gesture* and Bennington's 70-foot sloop *Mistral,* Sir Harry gave orders that she must answer the round-up each morning conducted by the Coast Guard cutter *Pindar,* which was accompanying the fleet; but refuse to give her position. Since the roll call was conducted by radio telephone, every ship in the fleet could listen to the reports of position and Sir Harry refused to give his rivals any information about how far ahead or behind them, to the north or to the south of them he lay, or how many miles he had made in a twenty-four-hour day.

Fair Maid actually was ahead of both his major rivals. She was seventy miles to the west of *Gesture,* which was also northward of her. By mid-passage she was eighty-five miles west of *Mistral* which, however, was fifty miles to the south and Diamond Head lying to the south and west, that eighty-five miles was not all gain. *Mistral* had had consistent winds. Taking a more southerly route at the start, she had picked up the trades a day earlier than *Fair Maid* and she was now gaining on her and the sail-tending and sail changes became more intense on the big yacht. Father Bredder was confused at the number of sails *Fair Maid* carried and the almost infinite variety of sail combinations that could be carried on her two masts. There were jibs and staysails, Genoas, mizzen staysails, spinnaker staysails and main and mizzen spinnakers. And of the spinnakers there were half a dozen for each mast, each different from its fellows in weight, cut and size and each suited then to a particular condition of the wind.

He suspected that sail changes were often ordered, particularly by Sir Harry, out of sheer nerves—out of brooding over *Gesture's* slight gain two days in succession and fretting over fancied faults in the cut of the particular sail being flown at that time. The helmsman was now relieved not every half hour but every twenty minutes, to keep him fresh. There was then, for the crew on watch, twenty minutes at the wheel and then an hour's rest before taking over a shift at the wheel again. And the work at the helm was made all the more harrowing because either Sir Harry or Larsen seated himself by the helmsman, watching for any error, ready to criticize as soon as a flaw, real or fancied, turned up in the steering.

Father Bredder endured this with patience. He was never allowed to finish his twenty minutes at the wheel now. Larsen invariably took over from him after criticizing his steering in a voice loud enough for the rest of the watch to hear. Because he was a humble man, the priest did not resent Larsen's abuse, but the case was altogether different with Smith, and between Smith and Larsen lay a smoldering resentment, likely to erupt under the strain at any moment.

The eruption came on the fifth day out when Smith, who had just taken over the wheel at the start of the watch, was spoken to abruptly by Larsen for being a little off the wind. Smith, his dark face even darker, got up from the helmsman seat, let go the wheel and said, "Steer the goddamn boat yourself." He let go the wheel and the *Fair Maid's* sails were fluttering as she rounded into the wind before Larsen got her back on course again. The Norwegian said nothing, but Smith wasn't through. "You say another word about my steering that isn't polite," he said, "and I'll stretch you on your back right here in this cockpit."

It was time for Father Bredder's watch to go below, and he did not hear the outcome of this particular incident. But the next time the watch changed, Smith took the wheel and Larsen did not say a word to him. An open rift had now been produced in the ship's community. It was a rift, Father Bredder reflected, that could have been closed by Sir Harry as owner and captain. But Sir Harry had not the respect of his ship's company. He was too interfering and too autocratic. He did not wield authority through superior character but through his position as owner, captain and multimillionaire. That was not enough to heal the breach.

So in mid-race, the tensions mounted on *Fair Maid*. Fredericks reserved his mockery for Sir Harry, whom he seemed to especially dislike. One day Sir Harry took a sight and when he had worked out his position, he was thirty-five miles south and east of that given by Fredericks. The navigator resented this interference in his department and did not fail to mention Sir Harry's error to the rest of the crew.

In this kind of atmosphere Father Bredder found some relief in his daily chat with Ben the cook. Ben now took a regular airing by popping his head through the forehatch and remaining for half an hour each noon with head and shoulders above the deck but never emerging any further. Ben told Father Bredder that he considered the deck was reserved for the "ship's gentlemen." He, being a paid hand, was one of the "ship's servants," and so should not mingle on the deck with the others.

Ben knew a lot about the sea and sailing and could explain many puzzling little details. Once Father Bredder mentioned that both he and Storey, on the watch from midnight to four in the morning, had seen a white light downwind of them though they could not judge how far away.

"It went on and off," said Father Bredder. "But it was there for only a few minutes—perhaps really only a few seconds. And then it was gone."

"What they call a ghost light," said Ben. "You see them often, particularly if you're alone."

"Ghost light?" repeated the priest. "What is that?"

"Well, some say it is a ghost. These seas are empty now. The steamers all follow one lane, just like going on one of them freeways outside Los Angeles. But not so long ago you'd see sailing ships day and night and in every part of this ocean. They didn't follow any narrow lane but sailed according to the wind. And those lights that you see, people say are the ghosts of those ships. But I don't believe it. I'll tell you what I think those lights are, if you'd like to hear. I've seen them many times myself."

"Certainly I would like to hear," said Father Bredder.

"Well, there's a lot of phosphorescence in the sea out here," said Ben. "You can see it along the ship's side and in her wake as she goes through the water. Now when a wave crests some distance off the ship—say maybe three or four miles away, and you see it at the right angle—then you'll see a flash that looks just like a masthead light. It's gone in a minute, of course. And then you don't know exactly where you saw it except that it was to leeward or to windward or off the bow, which is only a general direction. So you keep looking and soon you see another flash.

"Now it's a fact that when you get one big wave that crests, you'll get two or maybe three. And then no more. So you see these 'ghost lights,' as they call them, flash maybe twice and maybe three times. And then you don't see them again—not until there's another series of big waves and they catch your eye just right. And that's what it is in my opinion. Everybody's always looking for lights at sea anyway, and that makes you more liable to see them.

"I remember one time making this same crossing on a schooner called the *Double Eagle*. She was undermanned so that we just had one man at the wheel and nobody else on deck nights. Well, this young German was at the wheel and suddenly he shouts out that we're being run down by a steamer from aft. And up everybody comes on deck and sure enough there's the masthead light of a steamer right behind us and rushing down on us, or so it seemed. Only it wasn't a masthead light at all but only Venus coming up as big as if it were a ship's lantern half a mile off.'"

Ben now gave that look of his which was half blank stare and half cunning scrutiny about the deck and said in a lower voice, "This is the part of a voyage when the cook had better not make any mistakes."

"Why?" asked Father Bredder.

"We're halfway there," said Ben. "People are beginning to get their dander up with each other. Oh, I know. This isn't the first time I've cooked on a race. Sir Harry sent his whole breakfast back this morning. He always does that at the halfway mark. Cook's the easiest person to pick on when tempers are running a bit high. So I must watch my work now until we make Honolulu. Then everything will be hearts and flowers again."

"Have you been aboard with Sir Harry and Larsen before?" asked Father Bredder.

"Not on *Fair Maid,* of course," said Ben. "But his other boat, *Pendragon.* Yes. I sailed the Bermuda race with them and the Fastnet. That's sailed over in England."

"So they're well used to each other?" said the priest.

"There's some people never gets used to each other," said Ben. "And Sir Harry and Mr. Larsen are two of them. Sir Harry keeps Mr. Larsen because he's the best sailing master to be found. Everybody will tell you that. But they don't like each other and they don't have much regard for each other. Sir Harry don't like the fact that Mr. Larsen is a better sailor. And Mr. Larsen don't like the fact that since he's been with Sir Harry, he's never won a race yet."

"Never?" echoed the priest.

"No. Not one. And he won't win this one either."

"Why?"

"Matter of luck," said Ben. "Things always go wrong on Sir Harry's boat. We've had Clancy so far on this voyage, but that won't be the end of it. Whatever happens, *Fair Maid* won't be the first to cross the line at Honolulu. Sir Harry's got all the money that a man could want, but I got one thing he hasn't got and that he can't buy."

"What's that?" asked Father Bredder.

"Luck," said Ben. "He's the unluckiest man I ever met. And this here is a real unlucky ship. You just wait and see."

But Father Bredder did not believe in luck, and when

Ben had popped down below like a jack-in-the-box, having had his airing for the day, the priest considered what factors there might be that would lead to a man having a reputation for being unlucky. Someone—Minardi, in fact—had once referred to Sir Harry as a Jonah, and Father Bredder started going over in his mind the details of Jonah's story. He remembered the point about being swallowed by the whale very well, and finally being thrown up on some unnamed shore.

Jonah, it seemed to Father Bredder, had been somewhat hot-tempered and argumentative. Wishing to get all the points of the story straight, the priest went below to his bunk and found and brought on deck a compact pocket Bible in a modern translation to refresh his mind on the points of the story. He was surprised how much of the story he had forgotten. Jonah, sent to Nineveh to warn the people that God was aware of their wickedness, had instead sought to flee to the Phoenician city of Tarsish because he was sure he would not be listened to in Nineveh.

A storm had overtaken the ship and the sailors had all prayed to their gods, but Jonah slept below and was dragged on deck by the sailors, who demanded that he pray to his God also, to abate the rage of the wind and sea. Jonah then confessed that he could not pray, for he was running from his God, and the seamen were filled with terror that he should do such a thing. It was Jonah himself who had told them to throw him into the sea, and the seamen would not do so at first, but tried rowing the ship to shore. Only when this failed did they throw Jonah overboard, and then only with prayers that they be forgiven for killing him. That was something Father Bredder had forgotten.

Having read the story through, Father Bredder was immediately struck with how falsely it was interpreted. The word Jonah these days meant someone who brought bad luck. But this was merely the decay of religion into superstition. What was important about Jonah was that he had disobeyed God and tried to hide from him.

And Sir Harry?

Father Bredder did not know.

Twelve

A DAY LATER, with Honolulu scarcely eight hundred miles distant, the port watch to which Father Bredder belonged sat down for breakfast at seven in the morning. They were to relieve the starboard watch at eight and all were a little glum and sleepy, for they had been on duty scarcely three hours before and had had a bad watch of it, for the ship had run into a series of violent winds and rain squalls.

The breakfast was far better than Father Bredder ate ashore—orange juice, choice of cereal, bacon or ham and eggs, hot cakes, toast and a variety of jellies and preserves. The crew worked hard and slept only at random, but they ate well and regularly, and the smell of hot coffee freshly made did a little to brighten them up.

"Proper bastard of a night," said Storey, reaching for toast and butter. "Must be getting close to the big island. Always get these squalls on the approaches to Hawaii."

"I can smell the plumeria already, and the ginger lilies, or whatever they call them," said Moulter. "Also the mai tais and the whisky and soda and maybe even the hula girls—with all the deference to yourself, padre."

Father Bredder chuckled. "I'd have been worried if you didn't mention them," he said. "About how far off do you suppose we are? We were really traveling during our watch."

"Seven hundred and seventy-eight miles to Diamond Head," said Fredericks, putting in an appearance. "I got a nice star fix this morning at dawn. Put us about eight miles further south than the line of position showed. About noon, if the wind holds, I expect we'll jibe over to the starboard tack. It will be watch out for squalls from now on."

"What's our speed—average?" asked Storey.

"Shade over ten knots," said Fredericks. "Might be up to eleven knots for the twenty-four hours at noon. She's really rolling now."

The men at the breakfast table could both feel and hear that she was. Even below there was a sound half between a rumble and a hiss when *Fair Maid* caught a following sea and surfed along before it, bringing faintly heard cheers from the men in the cockpit. "On some of those waves she's showing seventeen knots," said Fredericks. "Smith's at the wheel and Larsen is keeping his mouth shut."

This remark was received in silence. The quarrel between Smith and Larsen was reckoned a starboard watch affair. Moulter glanced at his watch. "Five minutes, chaps," he said. "And then the fun starts. Time for one more cup of coffee."

Francis came to serve the coffee and looked so worried that Moulter asked him what was the matter. "It's Sir Harry, sir," said Francis. "He's sleeping very heavily. I've taken him his breakfast and he doesn't answer my knock."

"He was up half the night," said Storey. "Let him sleep. He's the owner."

"He gets angry if I let him oversleep," said the steward. "I don't know what to do."

Without a word Father Bredder left the table, pushed

past Francis, and went through the corridor under the cockpit to the door at the far end which led to Sir Harry's stateroom. He thumped on the door with his big fist and then, getting no reply, tried to open it. It was locked on the inside. The priest whirled around, dashed back down the short corridor, up the circular staircase to the deck and, almost knocking Larsen down, crossed the cockpit to the companionway leading from the deck to the Great Cabin. A chest-high door here, opening inwards, led down a flight of stairs into Sir Harry's cabin, and the priest thumped on this. Again there was no reply and the priest seized the knob and turned it savagely. The door opened and he scrambled down the stairway. One glance told him that the cabin was empty. He seized the door of the shower and pulled that open, but that compartment was empty also. He whirled about, lumbered back upstairs again and shouted to Larsen.

"Sir Harry's not in his cabin. Is he on deck?"

"No," said Larsen. "Isn't he below? Maybe he's up forward!"

"I don't know," said Father Bredder. "You'd better search the ship right now. I think something has happened to him."

Larsen, with one glance about the deck, disappeared below and Father Bredder followed him. He heard Larsen instruct Moulter and the others to search the ship for the knight, but he himself went once more into the corridor below the cockpit and this time pulled open the door of the engine room. But Clancy was alone in the compartment, checking the electrolyte in the storage batteries.

"What's the matter?" asked Clancy.

"Sir Harry's missing," said the priest, and dashed out to

return to the knight's cabin. He found Francis there, looking blankly about him.

"Have you touched anything?" asked the priest.

"No," said the steward. "I just can't believe that he's gone. He must be somewhere about the ship. I saw him only a little while ago."

"When?" demanded the priest.

"Just after five o'clock," said Francis. "He rang for me to bring him a pot of coffee. He had been on deck and he said he felt cold."

"Are you sure of the time?" the priest asked.

"It was ten minutes past five on the galley clock," said Francis. "I was watching the clock because Sir Harry is very particular about the amount of time his coffee is brewed."

"There was no one with him when you brought the coffee?"

"No, sir."

"Did he lock the door to the corridor after you left?"

"Yes, sir. He always locked that door."

"But he left the one to the deck open. Did he ever lock the one to the deck—ever lock himself in his cabin?"

Francis looked puzzled. "What would he want to do that for?" he asked.

Father Bredder ignored the matter for the time being. "If you were up about five o'clock, did you see Mr. Larsen?" he asked.

"No," said the steward.

"You didn't see him pass the galley on his way to his bunk?"

"No. I saw nobody but Sir Harry."

"What was Sir Harry wearing?"

"His pajamas. His blue silk pajamas."

"And a dressing gown?"

"No."

"Slippers?"

"Yes. He had on slippers. Those slippers there," pointing to a pair by the side of the bed. Father Bredder bent and put his hand into one of the slippers, but the interior was cool to the touch.

"Stay here and don't let anybody come in and don't touch anything," he said, and went out on deck. The rest of the crew were gathered in the cockpit. A search of the boat had revealed no trace of Sir Harry.

"You looked in the sail bins?" asked Larsen.

"Everywhere," said Moulter. "Even in the chain locker. We've searched every square inch of the ship and he isn't on board." The silence that followed that statement, broken only by the seethe and rumble of the sea and the hissing of the wind, seemed utterly desolate.

"We must go back," said Larsen. "Get the spinnakers off her and set the jib topsail and forestaysail. Fredericks, alert the *Pindar*. Tell them we have a man lost overboard, and give them our position now and our position at the time Sir Harry was last seen aboard."

"That was at ten minutes past five this morning," said Father Bredder.

Larsen grunted and turned to Yamashito, who was at the wheel. "Bring her round to the wind when the chutes are off her," he said. "Move!" Moulter had already gone forward to handle the main spinnaker halyard. Todd took the guy line off the cleat and Storey and Woods tailed on the sheet.

"All ready aft," shouted Todd.

"Here she comes," said Moulter and, standing back from

the mast, pulled the halyard away from the winch. There was a tremendous whirling of line and Storey and Woods started hauling in on the sheet as if possessed. The enormous tricolor sail, big enough to cover the whole ship, bellied out downwind and then, pulled by one corner, streaked in toward the cockpit. The men fought it in armfuls and Father Bredder took the end and led it down to the cabin where Ben, deserting his galley, snaked it down the circular staircase and commenced to stow it to one side.

Vast as it was, the sail was off the mast and down below in little over a minute. The mizzen spinnaker had not been set because of the violence of the squalls during the night. Before the new headsails were on the ship, Yamashito put the big wheel to windward and *Fair Maid* turned on her keel like a circus pony and for the first time since meeting the trades, faced the wind and the sea. The change in conditions on board was immediate and dramatic. *Fair Maid* no longer sailed on an even keel with a slight roll, but heeled far over and drove her bow like the cutting edge of a harpoon into the glistening blue waves that now raced down on them from the northeast. For a minute or two, until she got her headsails, *Fair Maid* seemed to make no headway. And then, with jib topsail and forestaysail set, she settled down to her business and the dial on the speedometer registered first four then six and then nine knots.

New as he was to sailing, Father Bredder had learned enough to know that the yacht could not sail directly into the wind. She would have to sail back the way she came, taking a zigzag course, constantly crossing the wind. In this way the ketch would follow a course that would average out to the direction from which she had come, but would by no means follow her precise track.

"Couldn't we use the engine?" asked the priest of Moulter, who had come back into the cockpit.

"No propeller," said Moulter. "Remember? It was taken off in Pedro."

"I think I could dive and put it on," said the priest.

"Just obey orders," said Moulter grimly. "This isn't the time for suggestions."

Everybody had by now come back into the cockpit, and Larsen said, "We have a good chance of finding him. At least a fifty-fifty chance. At farthest he may be forty-five miles upwind. We have maybe ten hours of daylight left and we can cover that distance easily. The main thing is spotting him. Everybody except the helmsman keep a sharp lookout. If you see anything at all, shout and point. And keep pointing even after we have got a compass bearing on whatever you have seen." He went below then to where Fredericks was working the radio telephone, remained awhile and returned.

"*Pindar* is coming and joining in the hunt and so are two Class B sloops, *Astarte* and *We're Alone*. *Gesture* and *Mistral* are abandoning the race and heading for the place where Sir Harry was last known to have been aboard. We will search back to that point. They will search from that point toward us. I want Fredericks to plot the whole situation for me, so he must be relieved at the radio telephone. You," turning to Father Bredder. "Can you operate it?"

"I think so," said the priest.

"Go down and tell Fredericks I want you to take over from him and have him show you what to do. Then send him up here."

Down went the priest and it seemed to him that Fredericks was annoyed at being relieved of the radio duty and was in no great hurry to get up to Larsen with the plotting sheets.

"Press the switch to talk," he said. "Resist the temptation to yak and remember that for some unknown reason the Coast Guard has to be told everything twice."

Father Bredder put the headphones on and looked over the high seas radio set, which it was actually illegal for him to use, though that would be overlooked in this emergency. There were a number of dials with hairlike needles quivering on them, but he decided to ignore all these and concentrate on the transmit switch and the microphone. He had hardly sat down before he heard, clearly and calmly, *"Pindar* calling *Fair Maid.* Over."

"Fair Maid to *Pindar. Fair Maid* to *Pindar,"* said Father Bredder. "I read you loud and clear. Over."

"Pindar to *Fair Maid.* We require EP and ET of accident. Repeat. Require EP and ET of accident. Over."

This Father Bredder, a little flustered, translated as a request for the estimated position and estimated time of Sir Harry's going overboard. He replied, in the required gobbledegook, that he would give the information when it was checked and, taking off the headphones, went to the cockpit to ask Fredericks.

"Goddamn Coast Guard," said Fredericks. "I just gave it to them. Tell them ET was 1500 hours Greenwich and EP 141. 20 west and 23.36 north. It's on that scratch pad."

Father Bredder returned to the radio telephone, where he found the information written on a scratch pad, gave it over the air and was then queried about the longitude again. He gave this once more. He was then asked to stand by and heard *Pindar* broadcast this information to the whole fleet and request again that all boats within a hun-

· *101*

dred miles of the position abandon the race and converge to join in the search. This amounted immediately only to the boats already contacted.

And then, over the air, came a message tapped out slowly in Morse. Father Bredder did not know Morse and waited patiently for the translation which came as follows, *"Emerald* to *Pindar. Emerald* to *Pindar.* I am forty-five miles southeast of estimated position of accident. Repeat. Am forty-five miles southeast of estimated position of man overboard. Am proceeding there under sail and engine. Estimate arrival in five hours. Estimate arrival in five hours. Batteries low and cannot transmit by voice. Over."

Larsen came below with Fredericks and entered the navigation room, which was directly opposite the well-equipped radio room in which Father Bredder was seated. The priest gave the information about *Emerald* to Larsen and he grunted and, entering the navigator's cabin with Fredericks, closed the door behind him.

Father Bredder settled down to his radio watch, his mind a whirl of questions and conjectures which he must bring sternly under control if he was to do the right thing.

And if he did not do the right thing, he realized, Sir Harry would drown.

Thirteen

ALL THAT FORENOON *Fair Maid* tacked back along her course toward the place where Sir Harry was last known to have been on board. Tacks were made every fifteen minutes precisely, and at each tack the yacht's position was marked by Fredericks on his plotting sheet. He now made two copies of this plot. One copy was for the Coast Guard cutter *Pindar* when he met with her so that he could show exactly the path taken by *Fair Maid* in her search and thus the area which had been scrutinized by her crew. This would avoid the same area being combed twice.

The second copy he put before Father Bredder, seated in the comfortable radio room opposite the navigation room. He explained to the priest how to mark the ship's position on this plotting sheet by the latitude and longitude supplied him at each tack. This turned out to be nothing more complicated than plotting a graph with two variables, the upright axis representing latitude and a horizontal axis longitude. The priest was able quite readily to keep track of *Fair Maid's* position and give this to *Pindar* and other vessels joining in the search when required. On the plotting sheet Fredericks had marked both the place where it had been discovered that Sir Harry was not aboard and the place where he was last known to have been aboard. Thus the priest, plotting each tack, could see how the ketch was working her way back toward the focal point of the search.

Others, summoned by the Coast Guard, now joined the search which had expanded from a local tragedy in a racing fleet to a matter of international concern and importance. A Lurline freighter, *Clematis,* said she was interrupting her voyage to Los Angeles to join the searchers. Another Coast Guard cutter, *Achilles,* equipped with a helicopter, had been dispatched from Honolulu at her full speed of 30 knots and search planes were being sent out from Honolulu—some said Navy, some said Army—to comb the waters where Sir Harry was believed to have gone overboard. In an hour, it seemed to Father Bredder, listening at the radio, the whole world had become conscious of this one man, lost in the ocean, and the whole world was hoping that he would be found.

The radio traffic became so great—for it included not only messages from the search vessels, but also messages from pilots of commercial aircraft flying over the area and messages from Los Angeles and Honolulu by radio telephone from worried presidents of companies of all kinds in which Sir Harry was interested—the traffic then became so great that *Pindar,* acting as communications center, designated one frequency as the channel to be used entirely for search reports and to this channel, then, Father Bredder switched, cutting out the clamor of the anxious world.

Everybody on *Fair Maid* was keyed up with the tension of the search. All knew that it was quite possible to pass within a hundred yards of Sir Harry, struggling for his life in the water, and not see him. The waves were not big— perhaps no more than five feet from trough to crest. But the fetch between crest and crest was huge, a valley in the ocean, between long liquid hills in which an object as small as a man could easily be missed. Because they knew this, and because every man visualized himself in Sir Harry's place, the crew watched the waters ahead, behind, to the sides, without cease and, refusing to eat below, Francis served them lunch of sandwiches on deck.

Yamashito and Todd, who were both men of lighter weight, volunteered to go up to the spreaders, the better to see. But Larsen withheld permission. In this kind of sea and with tacks being taken every fifteen minutes, the spreaders were no place for a lookout. Everybody stayed on deck, and when the helmsman was relieved at the end of each hour, he remained with the watchers. Nobody thought of a watch below—time off after four hours' duty.

The sun rose higher and with the ascending of the sun the wind quickened as it always did in these latitudes, the rising wind producing flumes and swatches of dazzling white on the exulting blue of the ocean. In the overpowering light eyes grew tired and smarted. People squinted and shaded their eyes with their hands. But they did not stop looking.

There were two false alarms when dark round objects were sighted. Each time *Fair Maid* headed toward them to discover, when a few yards off, that they were but the glass globes used by Japanese fishermen to float their deep-sea fishing lines. Yet there was encouragement in the fact that the globes were sighted, for this was a measure of the keenness of the watch from the decks of *Fair Maid*.

Even Ben came apologetically on deck to stare with his strangely blank eyes at the sea. But Ben was a professional seaman and inclined to pessimism.

"He's gone," he kept saying, shaking his head. "Money didn't help him. He hadn't any luck." Larsen eventually told Ben to get below, which he did, going down the aft stairway this time rather than popping down the forehatch as he normally did. This brought him past the radio room where Father Bredder was working and, having looked carefully about to see that he was not observed, Ben put his head through the door and said in a stage whisper, "It's all a waste of time. If you can't pick a man up within ten minutes of his going overboard, he's a goner. Once out of sight, he's lost."

"He might be found, Ben," said Father Bredder, who removed his earphones for this little conversation.

"Not a chance," said Ben. "And with his kind of luck, not a chance even if there was a chance; if you know what I mean."

Keeping the radio watch, Father Bredder had no opportunity to ponder the circumstances which had led to the disappearance of Sir Harry. He knew that he ought to be thinking about this—that there was something important in Sir Harry's stateroom which he had noted while questioning Francis, but whose significance had for the moment escaped him.

He was uneasy because of that odd something in the cabin, but with ship after ship coming on the air, and also some of the search planes, and with the demand for information from *Fair Maid* and the occasional need to relay a message from one ship to another, he had no time for speculation. So he sat at the radio, doing an important job, to be sure, but uneasily aware that there was something else which he should do and which just might lead to the rescue of Sir Harry before it was too late.

The navigator of the Coast Guard cutter *Pindar* had now prepared a search pattern for the various vessels which he transmitted and which would in effect cover the area where Sir Harry was believed to have gone overboard with a grid of searching ships. But whether this grid would be fully effective would depend on the ability of the skippers and navigators of the ships involved to find the station allotted to them and steer the course prescribed. In Frederick's opinion, all this was just Coast Guard foolishness, because a lot of the yachts would be lucky to be able to establish their own position within five miles with accuracy.

A little after midday *Emerald* came on the air again, transmitting once more in Morse, and the other ships fell silent while the slow procession of dots and dashes came through their receiver. Father Bredder listened, waiting for *Pindar* to acknowledge receipt of the message and translate it for the rest of the searchers. At last *Pindar's* radioman repeated the message by voice, both to check its accuracy and inform the rest of the fleet of its contents. He said:

"*Pindar* to *Emerald*. *Pindar* to *Emerald*. Your signal received as follows. Quote. Have found dressing gown of blue silk floating 23 10 north 141 10 west. Searching area. Unquote. Have I received you correctly? Over. *Pindar*."

Father Bredder did not wait for any further news. He unplugged the earphones and, with the cord dangling down before him, dashed up the stair to the cockpit.

"*Emerald* has come across a dressing gown floating in the water. Right here," he said, and thrust into Larsen's hand a leaf from the scratch pad on which he had noted down latitude and longitude.

Larsen stared at it a moment and, turning to the plotting sheet which Fredericks had before him pinned to a drawing board, said, "Check that position. Be sure it's absolutely right."

"Or as right as *Emerald's* navigator can make it," said Fredericks.

"You know him?" snapped Larsen.

"Yes. He's a good man. But you can't get absolute accuracy in this kind of a sea. Five miles off would be good. A circle with a radius of five miles covers an awful lot of water."

Father Bredder went below and waited for an interval in which to call *Pindar* and ask for a check on the position. But *Pindar* had anticipated the request and, having contacted *Emerald,* rebroadcast the position. She then announced that she was heading directly for the area and called on all boats to alter course to the new position which was now to become the focus of the search.

Father Bredder, using Francis as a messenger, sent the information to Larsen. Larsen replied with a scribbled note giving *Fair Maid's* estimated position at 141 48 west and 23 22 north, which the priest plotted on his chart and then transmitted to *Pindar.* He also plotted on the chart the positions of the other ships reporting so that he had before him a complete picture of the search.

Pindar was actually farthest from the focal point but, being capable of 30 knots, would get there in a little over two hours. *Emerald* was, of course, at the new focal point and tacking back and forth over the area in which the dressing gown had been found. *Fair Maid* was to the north and west and distant about twenty miles. She was close-hauled on the port tack and if, as the priest guessed, she was making eight knots then she would be at the focus in something under three hours.

The priest studied the pattern of the search and while he did so listened to the radio telephone reports. *Emerald* came back on the air this time in a voice broadcast to report that she had repaired her generator and that there was another sail in sight to the southwest. Then *Mistral* called *Pindar* to identify herself as the sail seen by *Emerald* and in a little while the two boats were searching together.

Fair Maid meanwhile clawed and knifed her way to windward, steering, Father Bredder could tell by the chart, a course of east southeast. He could see the spray fly past the porthole of the radio room and guessed that the crew above were in foul weather gear. Something troubled him about the position marked on the plotting sheet; something about which both Larsen and Fredericks must be aware. It was this: that the position in which the dressing gown had been found floating in the water was a good distance south—fifteen miles on the chart—of the position of *Fair Maid* when Sir Harry was last seen aboard. Not only south, but slightly to the east. And *Fair Maid* had been traveling to the west. So how could the dressing gown have gone fifteen miles or so at right angles to the ship's course? Perhaps it was not Sir Harry's dressing gown, but one that had been dropped overboard by another vessel.

Francis was standing by, acting as messenger, and Father Bredder, taking off his earphones, asked the steward whether Sir Harry's dressing gown had any positive identifying marks.

"Oh, yes," said Francis. "His monogram was on the breast pocket and the dressing gown had two small gold buttons on each cuff."

Without consulting Larsen, Father Bredder contacted *Emerald* and asked for a description of the dressing gown. He was aware of the rest of the fleet listening as the description came. It included the details of the monogram and

· *109*

the gold buttons. It was Sir Harry's dressing gown, then, without any doubt. Yet how had it got to that position—a position which must surely raise a question among the rest of the searchers once they compared it with *Fair Maid's* earlier course?

Todd now came to relieve the priest at the radio telephone and as soon as he had handed it over, Father Bredder called Francis and went with him to the Great Cabin through the corridor that led under the cockpit. He knew now what was wrong in that cabin—what was the disorder which had lain all morning unidentified in the back of his mind.

Father Bredder found on entering the Great Cabin that it had been completely tidied though he had told Francis to leave it as it was. "Who ordered you to tidy this place?" he asked.

Francis hesitated and then said, "Mr. Larsen, sir. I told him you said to leave it and he told me to go ahead and tidy it, that you were not in command."

"All right," said the priest. "Now try to answer my questions accurately, for a great deal depends on getting the truth now. Sir Harry's life may depend on it. Tell me. When you tidied the bed, did you find Sir Harry's pajamas?"

"No, sir," said Francis. "He had them on. They were not in the cabin."

"You are absolutely sure?"

"Absolutely."

"Now how about his slippers. Were they in the cabin?"

"Oh, yes, sir. You saw them yourself. Right by his bed."

"Sir Harry had several pairs of slippers?"

"Yes. They were in the cupboard."

"They are all there? Please make sure for me."

Francis, puzzled, went to the cupboard and after a few moments asserted that all Sir Harry's slippers were there.

"How about deck shoes?" asked the priest. "Is there a pair missing?"

Francis checked and said, "Yes. One pair is not here."

"All right," said Father Bredder. "Now, is there a pair of slacks and a pullover or a jersey of any kind missing? Please look very carefully, for this is very important."

Francis, after a search, reported that a pair of flannel slacks and a light blue cashmere pullover were gone. The priest made him check, but he could not find these items.

"That is what I wanted to know," said Father Bredder, and went on deck to see Larsen.

"We are headed to the wrong place to find Sir Harry," he said. "Sir Harry was not wearing that dressing gown when he went overboard."

"What the hell do you mean he wasn't wearing the dressing gown?" demanded Larsen. "It's his, isn't it? And it was found over the side."

"Yes," said the priest. "But it was thrown over the side to mislead the searchers. Somebody on board tried to murder Sir Harry. It may still be possible to save him. But he will not be found anywhere near that dressing gown."

Fourteen

"YOU WILL HAVE to listen closely to what I have to say to follow me," said Father Bredder. "I am not very good at explanations. But I will do my best. It will help if you don't interrupt."

Larsen, seated in the Great Cabin, said, "Get on with it. What have you got on your mind?"

"The first point is that Sir Harry was not wearing that dressing gown when he went over the side," said the priest.

"How do you know?" Larsen demanded.

"You will recall that I was the first one to discover that Sir Harry was not in his cabin," said the priest. "I had suspected that something might have happened to him and when Francis said he was difficult to wake, I went immediately to his cabin and found it empty. The bed had been slept in, there were no pajamas lying on it, but Sir Harry's slippers were on the floor by the bed. The slippers are very important.

"At first I didn't realize myself the importance of the slippers, and I was too busy with the radio this morning to think about it, though I knew that there was something wrong connected with them. It was not until we got *Emerald's* report of finding that dressing gown—and I myself

112 ·

checked that it was indeed Sir Harry's dressing gown—that I knew what was wrong. The circle was incomplete."

"Circle?" said Larsen.

"It is a figure I picked up from Moulter," said the priest. "There are three items of bedroom clothing that go together—pajamas, slippers, and a dressing gown. A man who wears a dressing gown over his pajamas to go on deck would also wear his slippers. Pajamas, dressing gown, slippers—they go together, and Sir Harry Stockton was the kind of man who would not break that combination."

"So?" said Larsen.

"So the combination was broken," said the priest. "The circle was bent. The slippers were left on board, here in Sir Harry's cabin. But the dressing gown was found in the ocean."

"Good God," cried Larsen. "Do you mean that it is because of this kind of drivel you conclude that somebody tried to murder Sir Harry?" He rose to go, but the priest held out a hand to detain him.

"There's something else," he said. "Sir Harry decided to go on deck for some reason. He would normally have put on his dressing gown and his slippers—you have seen him do so many a time. But the weather was bad last night. So, instead, he put on a pair of gray flannel slacks over his pajamas and a blue cashmere pullover and also a pair of deck shoes. And then he disappeared. And my suspicions would not have been raised had it not been for the dressing gown being found in the water. Because Sir Harry Stockton would certainly never put a dressing gown over his slacks and pullover which had been put over his pajamas. For one thing it was not that cold last night. For another, the combination would offend him—it would not occur to him. If he wanted further protection, he would have used a light overcoat—of which there are two in that closet.

"It boils down to this. He was pushed overboard and whoever did this also threw his dressing gown overboard and some distance away to mislead the searchers."

"Has it occurred to you that Sir Harry might have lost the dressing gown overboard himself?" said Larsen. "He might have taken it off while he was on the deck earlier that night. It might have been blown overboard in the wind. Has that occurred to you?"

"Yes," said Father Bredder. "But I cannot believe such a thing. An experienced sailor like Sir Harry does not have something blow overboard. He does not put it down somewhere on deck where it will blow overboard. Nor would he take off his dressing gown on deck if the wind was blowing that hard in the first place."

But Larsen was by no means convinced. "It's quite possible," he said, "that Sir Harry put that dressing gown over his slacks and pullover. And it is also possible that he put on deck shoes instead of slippers because the decks were a little wet with dew and he didn't want to get his slippers wet."

Father Bredder nodded. "The decks were wet," he said. "They were wet and slippery. But Sir Harry chose his slippers for this voyage with that in mind. They have the same soles—though lighter—as deck shoes. He often put them on when going on deck at nighttime."

"All right," snapped Larsen. "But this time he didn't. And you've invented a whole cock-and-bull story out of nothing that could completely destroy the morale of my crew. So don't say another word about it to anyone. I believe that Sir Harry slipped and went overboard; that he was wearing that dressing gown at the time, and I am going to concentrate my search on the area in which the dressing gown was found."

He had his hand on the cabin door before the priest stopped him. "There's one other factor which you will have to explain to the Coast Guard even if you don't care to explain it to me," he said.

"And what's that?" demanded Larsen.

"Why Fredericks gave a wrong position for the ship at the time Sir Harry was last seen aboard," said the priest. "The position he gave was at least fifteen miles north of where Sir Harry's dressing gown was found."

"I'm going to tell you one thing and then I'm going to order you to keep your mouth shut about your suspicions. The thing I am going to tell you is this. With the sun directly overhead at midday—in fact a little to the north of us—no navigator can place his latitude with any great degree of accuracy. And now I am warning you—say nothing of this nonsense to anyone else on board and do not let me hear of you questioning any of the crew. When we meet with *Pindar,* I will make up my mind what to do about you."

With that he left, and Father Bredder sat down on Sir Harry's bed deeply disturbed. He was disturbed not because his own esteem was offended but because he had failed to direct the search to the place at which Sir Harry would most likely be found. He had failed utterly. All the search vessels were going to the wrong location and if Sir Harry was found it would be the result of—he almost said—an accident.

Where was Sir Harry most likely to be in relation to the present focus of the hunt? Upwind to the east? Or downwind to the west? In short, had the dressing gown been thrown overboard before or after the attempted murder? Unless this was a well-thought-out plan, most likely after the murder, the priest decided. It was the kind of detail that might occur to the murderer in coming across the dressing gown. He might see the dressing gown in Sir Harry's cabin and decide that it provided a good way of misleading the searchers on the time and the location of the crime.

However, for this scheme to succeed the murderer would have to allow a considerable time to pass before putting the dressing gown over the side—two hours would provide a safe margin, maybe, with the ship traveling at ten knots, for that would put the search twenty miles away from the proper place. Yet surely there was a huge element of chance in this business of waiting two hours, because two hours from five o'clock in the morning when Sir Harry was known to be on board would make it broad daylight. And there was a chance that Sir Harry's disappearance would be discovered earlier. No. It was more likely that the dressing gown had been thrown over before the murder.

Sir Harry was last seen on board at about five in the morning. That was the central fact that the priest knew he must keep firmly in mind. All right. If the dressing gown had been thrown overboard two hours before—at three o'clock—it would have been found about twenty miles eastward of its position. The priest realized, though not as fast as he should have, that the location of the dressing gown showed when it had been put overboard. It was, in fact, located on the same longitude, but about fifteen miles south of where Fredericks had said the ship was at five in the morning. So it had been thrown overboard about that time. And if he was correct in his theorizing, then Sir Harry had been murdered about two hours after that—seven in the morning.

In broad daylight?

Ridiculous. He was quite wrong. He was altogether wrong. The dressing gown and Sir Harry had gone overboard at the same time. In short, he had been wearing the dressing gown, and therefore the place where it was found was the place to search for him.

And yet, having come to this conclusion, which seemed unavoidable, Father Bredder was not comfortable with it. He was convinced that Sir Harry had not been wearing the dressing gown. He was convinced—or at least he was very strongly of the opinion—that the knight had gone overboard sometime after the dressing gown. But how would it be possible for a murderer in broad daylight to push him off the ship?

Father Bredder was still in the Great Cabin alone. He had not had any opportunity of searching it and he decided he should do so now. He would not be looking for anything in particular but for oddities which might suggest a profitable line of investigation.

One oddity struck him immediately. There were two large portholes on each side of the cabin and they were all closed tight so that the air was a little stuffy. There were two ceiling ventilators of a type which would permit air to come into the cabin but not water. He held his hand up to the ceiling grids but felt no influx of air. Perhaps, he decided, the cowls on the deck were not turned in the right direction to catch the wind. He could check that later. He opened the frosted sliding glass door of the stall shower. All was gleaming here, everything spotless; so spotless, in fact, that a slight discoloration around the drain attracted the priest's eye. His big fingers would not go between the openings of the drain to investigate this discoloration, but he got a slight smudge on the end of one, black and greasy, which he could not immediately identify.

He assumed that it was some kind of grease which had been used in tightening up the drain fitting and ensuring that the joint was watertight.

He next explored Sir Harry's desk, at which he had seen him writing in that journal with the blue leather covers. But the desk was locked and he did not think he had a right to force it. A medicine cabinet over the washbasin (equipped with gold faucets, as were the faucets in the shower) had a huge array of small bottles containing pills. One of them, a bottle of aspirin, was open. He found the screw-on cap on the shelf beside it.

That, and the dark smudge obtained from the drain of the shower stall, were the only oddities an hour's search of the Great Cabin produced. They suggested nothing immediately and, disheartened both at his failure to convince Larsen and the poor results of his search, the priest went on deck.

He arrived just in time to hear Francis shout, as he scrambled up the circular stairs to the cockpit, "They've found him! They've found him! Here," he thrust a scrap of paper into Larsen's hand.

Larsen glanced at the paper and then looked at the priest.

"Where?" demanded Father Bredder.

"You were right," Larsen said bitterly. "About twenty miles downwind of where the dressing gown was found."

Fifteen

SIR HARRY was dead. He had been found by watchers aboard the Lurline freighter *Clematis* and would perhaps not have been discovered at all but for two booby birds or Laysan albatrosses which were hovering around him. Their actions had attracted attention and it was seen that there was something in the water below them. Sir Harry was indeed barely afloat. The waves washed over him in callous succession. The doctor aboard *Clematis* had hardly to take a look before pronouncing him dead. He gave it as his opinion that he had been dead at least an hour and possibly three hours.

The news, broadcast to the searching yachts, was picked up and rebroadcast by others, including ham radio operators in both Hawaii and on the continental United States. Within a matter of minutes Sir Harry's death was known to the world over radio and television. And back came a flood of messages and questions directed to the Coast Guard, to *Clematis* and to *Fair Maid* and coming from bankers and boards of directors and newspapers and television stations and brokers and lawyers—a barrage of almost hysterical inquiry which included a demand for details from three United States Senators and five members of the British House of Commons—such was the impact on the worlds of finance and of politics of the death of the English knight.

In the midst of this deluge a message struggled through to Father Bredder. It was received by *Pindar,* whose plodding and unshakable radio operator, ignoring the pleas of the mighty for news, transmitted it loyally to *Fair Maid.* The message, written down by Todd, who still had the radio duty, read, *"Fair Maid* Attention Father Joseph Bredder Investigate fullest. Will meet you in Honolulu Minardi LAPD Homicide." There was a further message from Redwood directed both to the captain of *Pindar* and to Larsen. It requested that their complete cooperation be given to Father Bredder in his investigations into the death of Sir Harry.

Larsen did not really need that message. At the first report of the finding of Sir Harry, twenty miles from the place the dressing gown had been discovered, he realized that he had better listen to the big priest, whom he still did not like. He realized that he had better do this because if he did not, he would bring down heavy suspicion on himself. And he realized that in any case, as captain now of *Fair Maid,* his was the responsibility of finding out exactly how Sir Harry had been lost overboard—whether by accident or by design. It was plain that the news dealt him a heavy blow, but he was seaman enough to think first of his ship.

No sooner, then, had the news been broken than he turned to Moulter, who had the helm, and said, "Two forty. We will continue on to Honolulu."

"Two forty," said Moulter.

"Stand by to jibe," said Larsen. Moulter spun the wheel and the ketch fell off the wind, slumped horridly for a moment in a trough between two waves, and then, turning her stern across the wind so as to point her bows for the Hawaiian Islands, caught the trades on her starboard quarter. Mizzen, main and jib sails were slacked off and Larsen

120 ·

answered Yamashito's look by saying, "Yes. Get the number one Genoa on her and the mizzen staysail. No spinnakers. We are not racing any more. But I want to get to Honolulu in a hurry."

Father Bredder helped with the sails, feeling perhaps more than the others the sense of heavy loss which had now descended on the ship. He had known that he should watch Sir Harry ever since Clancy had nearly died in the engine room. And he had failed to keep a close enough watch on him. The Englishman's death, then, was in some measure his fault.

Meanwhile Todd had informed *Pindar* that *Fair Maid* was continuing to Honolulu and received the news that *Clematis* had agreed to carry Sir Harry's body to Los Angeles. Requests for details were still crowding in on *Clematis*, on *Pindar*, on *Gesture*, *Emerald*, *Mistral*, and *Fair Maid*. *Pindar* finally issued a statement which in effect clamped down on any further information being given out and required all ships to abide by this decision. But the world news industry was not to be headed off so readily. The pressure mounted for more information and particularly for information on how it was that the knight's dressing gown had been found so far distant from his body.

Pindar finally turned to Father Bredder on *Fair Maid* for comment on this. And Father Bredder replied without guile that this proved that the two had not gone overboard at the same time. His statement contained the inference that there was then no connection between these two things and for a while it abated the clamor for details.

Father Bredder, once the ship was again on its way to Honolulu, was not entirely grateful to Minardi for his message. He had won his point (though at a horrible price) with Larsen, and he would have preferred to continue his investigation quietly in the three days remaining before *Fair Maid* reached Honolulu. Since that was now out of the question, he decided to go boldly about the more obvious part of his inquiries and arranged with Larsen to interview each member of the crew separately with a view to finding out from them when they had last seen Sir Harry aboard, and what they and he had been doing at the time. This, the priest realized, was by no means a brilliant approach. But he consoled himself that he was not a brilliant man. He could not fly, so he had to plod. He started his plodding numbingly conscious of the fact that there were things such as motive and opportunity and past history which should also be investigated and that now was the precious time for such investigation, before alibis could be thought up and incriminating clues removed.

He had an advantage in knowing that the murderer was on board. But he was at a serious disadvantage in that the murderer, confined to the scene of the crime, could watch his chance to destroy incriminating evidence. And he, Father Bredder, could not stay awake day and night, watching eleven men.

Eleven? Yes, eleven. He himself made twelve and Sir Harry had been thirteen. He wondered how long it would be before somebody aboard—perhaps Ben—would stumble on that significant number.

The priest started his investigation with Fredericks. He had spoken of murder to Larsen, but he told Larsen that he would not speak of it to the others, and for this Larsen was grateful.

When Fredericks came to see him (these interviews were all conducted in Sir Harry's Great Cabin), Father Bredder wanted to know about the discrepancy between the position of the ship and the position in which the dressing gown had been found.

"There are two possible explanations," said Fredericks. "You can take your own choice among them, though I will tell you which I think is more likely.

"The first is a combination of navigator's error and the effect of wind, currrent, and surface drift. I've told you already that it is possible for a navigator on a small ship—and *Fair Maid* is by ocean standards a small ship—to be as much as five miles out in his position. This can result from a number of factors all producing an imperfect shot of the sun.

"One factor is the chance of using a false horizon instead of the true horizon in measuring the sun's angle. If, for instance, the rim of the sun in the sextant is brought down on the back of a wave instead of on the horizon, then an error occurs. Again, if the sextant is held slightly out of the vertical position, an error will occur. To avoid such errors—really to reduce them to a minimum—when approaching land I take a series of sights, all timed, and then take an average of the angles and an average of the times. There is still an error, of course. But it may be of less than a mile. However, out at sea, where there are no hazards, I am content with one good shot of the sun.

"Now you will notice that the dressing gown was to the south of the ship. In these latitudes in midsummer, it is extremely hard to get an accurate latitude sight. That sight is taken at exact local noon when the sun has reached its meridian. With the sun overhead, unfortunately, or nearly overhead, it passes through its meridian in a matter of seconds. It actually seems to zoom from one side of the ship to the other, and so the noon sight cannot be relied on. It is possible, however, to get latitude by taking a sight shortly before the sun reaches its meridian and shortly after. Then two circles result and the place where they intersect is the latitude of the ship."

He went on with his explanation, but Father Bredder did not follow it. "The distance between the ship's plotted position and the position in which the dressing gown was found, then, can be accounted for by acceptable errors in navigation?" he asked.

"Yes. Mine and those of the navigator on *Emerald*. He could be out a mile or two also. Let us suppose I was out two miles and he was out two miles. That makes four miles. The dressing gown would then be only ten or eleven miles out. And that could be accounted for by wind and surface drift and current. Surface drift, by the way, is the motion of the surface water caused by wind and wave action. It can run contrary to current, which is caused largely by the rotation of the earth."

"What about the other reason to account for the difference in positions?" asked the priest.

"That would be an error in my sextant," said Fredericks. "I favor the first reason. I had my sextant checked by the Southwest Instrument Company in San Pedro. They are first-class. And I'm very careful with it. We can always check the sextant when we get ashore in Honolulu. But I am sure it is accurate."

"The morning Sir Harry disappeared you said you had got a star sight," said Father Bredder. "At what time was that?"

"Five thirty-seven," said Fredericks. "I can give you the exact time down to the second because, of course, I had to time the sight."

"It was just dawn then?"

"Yes. It was exactly the right time for such a sight. I came on deck at five-fifteen because I needed a star fix. A fix, by the way, is the crossing of sights from two stars. I needed a fix because I had for three days been unable to get a satisfactory noon sight. For the reasons I have just explained. I knew our longitude, but I could not be sure of our latitude. I got a fix from Antares and Arcturus. It worked very nicely." Fredericks' pleasure in the fix showed even now.

"Did you see Sir Harry come on deck?" asked the priest.

"No. I think Yamashito was at the wheel. In fact, I know he was because I told him I was going to try for a sight, and to shout if it looked like a sea was going to board us. They were running a little big that morning. It had been a rough night."

"Yes," said Father Bredder. "We had got into the area of squalls. Who else was on deck that you actually saw?"

"I can't say that I actually saw any individual," said Fredericks. "There was someone in the cockpit with Yamashito. And I think two other hands over on the starboard side and about amidships. I was aware of them only as figures—not as individuals. I went forward myself, away from the cockpit, because in taking a star sight it is necessary to get the eyes accustomed to the darkness—so that the iris opens wide. Also if there is any reflected light from anywhere—the binnacle light, for instance, or a light from a cabin or even the navigation lights—the mirrors pick it up and it is hard to find either your star or the horizon. Star sights are quite difficult actually. Lots of navigators never bother with them for that reason."

"You came on deck about five-fifteen," said the priest. "But you did not take your sight until five thirty-seven?"

"Right," said Fredericks. "That was when I got the last shot—Arcturus. I left Arcturus to last because he is brighter and so would take longer fading from the sky which was, of course, growing brighter all the time."

"You saw no trace of Sir Harry?"

"None."

"Do you think he could have come on deck without your seeing him?"

"Certainly," said Fredericks. "After all, I was looking through the sextant. I hadn't time for looking around the decks."

"Where were you standing when you took the sight?" asked the priest.

"Right in the eyes of the ship—up in the bows," replied Fredericks. "I had to hold onto the jib stay to steady myself."

"Why so far forward?" asked Father Bredder.

"Because of the sails," said Fredericks. "That was the only position I could get a clear sweep from directly overhead down to the horizon without a sail intervening."

"You didn't hear anything or see anything suspicious?"

"Not a thing," said Fredericks.

"Have you ever seen any ghost lights at sea?" asked Father Bredder.

"Ghost lights?" echoed Fredericks. "What are they?"

The priest explained and Fredericks laughed. "No," he said. "I've never seen any. Nor the Flying Dutchman either."

When Fredericks had gone, Father Bredder recalled that

the navigator had said that the star sight put the yacht about eight miles south of the previous position. So that Fredericks' total error had been about twenty-three miles, fifteen miles plus eight miles. That was surely too much to ascribe to acceptable chance. The conclusion was unavoidable that Fredericks had deliberately misreported the yacht's position for some days. The priest decided to say nothing of this, even to Fredericks, for the time being.

Sixteen

THE QUESTIONING of the other members of the crew—a police procedure which Father Bredder did not like though he felt obliged to carry it out for Minardi—revealed that Francis was the last person to have seen Sir Harry. He had, as the priest knew, taken him a pot of coffee at ten minutes past five on the morning of his murder. He was the only one who had entered the Great Cabin that morning other than Sir Harry, and he was plainly afraid that this might incriminate him. He assured the priest that Sir Harry had been perfectly well and sitting on his bed when he left him with the coffee and said Sir Harry had always been a good employer, that he had been in his service for close to a dozen years, and he could gain nothing at all from his death but unemployment.

Such anxiety, far from making Father Bredder suspicious, roused his sympathy for Francis, who was evidently a man prone to misfortune and to victimization, lacking, it seemed, the virility of mind or muscle to defend himself. In his anxiety to prove his innocence, he put things in such order as to direct suspicion on himself, bringing out exactly the detail which others, more knowing, would either forget to mention or gloss over.

Thus Francis, emphasizing that he had no motive for

doing any harm to Sir Harry, said he owed the knight eight hundred dollars and was paying it back by regular deductions from his salary.

"Why had he had to borrow so large a sum?" asked the priest.

"It wasn't exactly borrowed," said Francis, and then tumbled out an untidy tale of needing several hundred dollars for an operation for his daughter and, desperate for money, taking a little here and a little there; selling a pair of cuff links of gold and an expensive pen, and so on, until Sir Harry had found the whole thing and threatened him with imprisonment. Then Sir Harry had relented and allowed him to repay the money from his salary.

Something about the British medical system occurred to Father Bredder and he asked whether the operation that Francis' daughter required was not covered by the socialized medical program of that country. No, it wasn't, Francis said. And, pressed, he admitted that the money was needed to pay an abortionist. The expression of grief on the priest's face at this news was not lost on Francis and he said passionately, "That baby would have ruined her life. She couldn't take care of it and neither could I." And then he added, almost in justification, "It would have been a girl."

Father Bredder was so shaken by this confession that he had difficulty continuing with his questioning. He could not readily acquit himself of guilt in this horrid little tale of infanticide, for although it was true, he lived thousands of miles from Francis, yet was it not also true that the same kind of thing was happening daily around him in Los Angeles—while he, a minister of God, took voyages on racing yachts and played detective?

He next questioned Francis about the dressing gown.

Francis didn't want to talk about this. He said at first that he had not missed it from the cabin. He said he thought Sir Harry had put it on when he brought him his coffee. Then realizing perhaps that this was a blunder, since the two had been twenty miles apart in the ocean, he said that he wasn't telling the truth. The fact was that the dressing gown had been missing the previous evening. Sir Harry had wanted to put it on after dinner (which he had taken in his cabin) but could not find it. He had accused Francis of making off with it. Francis had assured him he had not done so—that he had last seen it lying on an armchair.

"I believed he had hidden it on purpose," said the steward. "He did that sometimes after he had found out about me taking things. He would hide something and then make me sweat about it and accuse me of having stolen it. And then it would turn up, and I knew that he'd known where it was all the time."

This was a decidedly mean streak in Sir Harry that the priest had not suspected before. It surprised him. He knew the man to be an intolerable egotist. But he had not thought him a bully to his servants.

No one on the starboard watch—that is to say the watch which had had the duty from four in the morning to eight, had seen Sir Harry after he went below a little before five to turn in. The watch was supposed to work as a unit, but actually it tended to subdivide, as indeed did the port watch. Thus Yamashito and Smith, the watch captain, were most often together, and Todd and Clancy. It was Todd and Clancy, Father Bredder inferred, that Fredericks had seen as presences rather than as individuals up forward and on the starboard side when he went to take his star sights.

On the port watch, headed by Moulter and to which

Father Bredder belonged, nobody had seen Sir Harry since the change of watch at four in the morning. He had then conferred briefly with Larsen; Larsen had gone below warning of squalls and suggesting that they might change to a smaller spinnaker—a suggestion that Sir Harry had put aside with a measure of contempt. This left only Ben and Larsen to question. Larsen confirmed having seen Sir Harry at four in the morning at the change of watch and having spoken to him about the spinnaker change.

Father Bredder recalled that some days earlier, in the calm when he had first been entrusted with the wheel, he had heard what sounded like a quarrel between Larsen and Sir Harry. He asked Larsen about it.

"It was nothing," said Larsen. "It concerned sailing; nothing personal in the least."

"In what way did it concern sailing?" asked the priest.

"In a general way," said Larsen. "That was pretty early in the voyage—maybe three days out. He kept making sail changes without consulting me. He was working the crew too hard too early." Larsen fixed his pale blue eyes on the priest and said, with intensity, as if repeating the creed of his religion, "A good sailor sails for now and for an hour from now. A bad sailor sails only for now. Sir Harry was a bad sailor. Because he was a bad sailor and because he would not trust his sailing master—which was me—he lost all his races. He had no feel for weather—for the temperament of the wind. 'Get up the biggest sails you can carry and hold onto them.' That was as far as his sailing went. He would never have won. Even if he had not been killed, he would never have won. He could only see now. He could not see what was coming. After this voyage I was through with him anyway. Now he has ruined me, getting himself killed. I will bear the responsibility. You will see. Because I was the sailing master."

There was no mistaking the intensity of Larsen's feelings—his contempt, even hatred for Sir Harry.

"Why did you stay in his employ?" asked the priest.

"Money," said Larsen. "There aren't many who can pay two thousand dollars a month American for a sailing master. I will tell you another reason why he couldn't sail. It was because he wouldn't listen. Not that he wouldn't listen to me. But he wouldn't listen to the wind or listen to the sea. They have voices, too, you know."

"Have you ever lost a man overboard before?" asked the priest.

"Yes," said Larsen. "Three times. But they were found alive. There has always been an alarm. Once we nearly had one drown, though. He went overboard in the dark. Nobody knew he was gone until he was missed an hour later. He was a fool—like Sir Harry."

"In what way a fool?" asked the priest.

"A man who thinks he knows everything, who believes he can do everything better than everybody else, who is always checking to see that what others have done is done properly is a fool," said Larsen. "Sir Harry was always doing that. You want to know how I think he went overboard? Well, I think he lay in the cabin wondering about the set of the spinnaker; or maybe even wondering whether in view of the squalls he should not take my advice and change to a smaller sail. So instead of trusting his crew and the watch captain, he goes to take a look at the spinnaker himself. But he has to sneak up there to do it. If he can sneak up there, look at the spinnaker, find some fault, get back to his cabin and then come on deck to report that he thinks there is something wrong with the spinnaker, he has scored on the crew—see? You don't like that explanation—huh? Well, I knew him. And he was the greatest player of that English game that I ever met. You know the game I mean—Oneupmanship. Yes. He was the greatest player of Oneupmanship of any man I ever met. So he went forward and it was gusting hard, and the helmsman was having a hard time falling off before the wind when the gusts hit. So he's up there alone and the helmsman falls off a little and Sir Harry is taken off guard and goes over the side. And he could have screamed blue murder and nobody would ever have heard him in the wind and the sea noise."

"How could he have gone up forward without being seen?" asked the priest.

"Very simple," said Larsen. "The way he always did. By that door leading from his cabin to the corridor under the cockpit. That's how."

"That door was locked," said the priest. "I checked it myself."

"So Sir Harry had the key," said Larsen. "He could get back in when he wanted. He always kept it locked."

"You think he might have gone forward below deck and then got on deck through that forehatch?"

"Yes," said Larsen. "It wouldn't be the first time he did that. He didn't lead his crew. He competed against them. He spied on them."

"Would it be that easy for him to go overboard really?" asked Father Bredder. "He was, after all, thoroughly experienced on yachts."

"Look," said Larsen. "There is a rule that goes for all ocean-racing yachts and it is this—never send one man forward at night. Always two. Now that rule is there because it is easy for one man to go overboard. Decks are slippery. You cannot see lines that are lying about. Lines can come off cleats and lie about the deck unseen in the darkness. Step on one and it's like stepping on a roller skate. Over you go. The fool like Sir Harry that we lost in the Fastnet went over so quick that when we picked him up he had a dislocated hip—from trying to get his balance as his legs went from under him. And that is my opinion on how Sir Harry was lost. Murder is your opinion. But I believe an accident."

"There's the dressing gown," said the priest.

"Ask Francis about that," said Larsen. "He will tell you that Sir Harry had a funny habit of hiding things to watch others sweat."

"You mean he might have thrown it overboard himself?" asked the priest.

"It went over before he did and it was his dressing gown," said Larsen. "For murder you have to have a motive. Everybody on board this ship disliked Sir Harry Stockton. Maybe if you put all that dislike into one man you might have enough to make him a murderer. But it was divided among twelve men. He died in an accident. Of that I am certain. Just as certain as I am that I will be blamed for it. Not among sailors. No. Not among them. But among those who hire sailors, yes. There won't be many running to hire Sven Larsen for sailing master for a while."

When he had left, Father Bredder reflected that if there was one man aboard who stood to lose by the death of Sir Harry, it was the sailing master of *Fair Maid*. Far from having a motive for killing Sir Harry, he had a very strong motive for keeping him alive.

Seventeen

LARSEN'S THEORY of accidental death did not convince Father Bredder, but it explained how Sir Harry could have got unobserved from his cabin to the deck. That night when he was on watch, he tested the route. Storey was at the wheel and Moulter and Woods were in the cockpit. The priest slipped below and, starting from Sir Harry's door at the end of the corridor, went forward belowdecks to the forehatch. He passed the starboard watch, all asleep in their bunks forward of the main salon. But nobody stirred. He found the forehatch which opened up from a large compartment called the sail locker. This compartment ran completely across the ship and had on each side a number of bins in which the many sails of *Fair Maid* were stowed. The hatch was locked, for the ship was once again running through rain and wind squalls. But a ladder made it easy to pull the locks and open the hatch. The priest did this and emerged on the deck.

He had stood on this spot many times before talking with Ben. He looked about now, visualizing the situation with Fredericks up forward in the eyes of the ship taking a star sight. It was plain that Sir Harry, if he had indeed come up the forehatch, would not have been seen by the navigator, for the big spinnaker staysail would lie between them.

Equally Sir Harry was not likely to have been seen by the afterguard in the cockpit, for he would be thirty feet or more from them, in the predawn gloom, and with the huge boom of the mainsail impeding though not entirely cutting off the view.

He glanced backward toward the starboard or right-hand side of the ship where Fredericks had said he saw two figures standing. Sir Harry could have been seen by them, all right, if they happened to be looking in the direction of the hatch. But men on watch at sea look out to sea, and so it was possible that if Sir Harry had come on deck through this hatch, he had not been observed by anyone.

Before returning to the cockpit, Father Bredder looked about at the magnificence of the sky. Among the myriads of stars overhead there were several which blazed so brightly as to be almost three-dimensional. There was one very large star, almost overhead of the vessel, an emperor of light among mere kings. Surely, the priest thought, that must be one of the stars that Fredericks had used as his fix on that morning.

In the blaze of stars the Big Dipper was a little difficult to pick out. Northward of it, close to the horizon, he saw two other large stars each almost the peer of the imperial beauty overhead. Before returning to the cockpit, he went up to the eyes of the ship. Here he had an unimpeded view to the north and the east, but southward the tremendous Genoa obliterated the sky and the ocean. Of course when Fredericks had been taking his sight, the spinnaker had been up, ballooning out over the bow supported to windward by the long spinnaker pole with all its tackle. With that sail set the sky and the ocean from southwest to northwest was gone. The star overhead could still be seen, but only the more eastward of the two large stars which were closer to the northern horizon. The motion in the bows of the boat—a tremendous surge forward and down followed by a slow and somewhat nauseating lift of the bow through several feet—made the priest a little uncomfortable and he returned to the cockpit.

"Hello," said Moulter, who had the wheel, "I was beginning to wonder where you were. Thought we might have another man overboard. What have you been up to?"

"I was trying to find out whether I could get forward without being seen by anyone on deck or below."

"And you could?"

"Yes," said the priest. "Do you know anything about the stars?"

"Try me," said Moulter.

"Which is Arcturus?"

"Can't miss it," said the Englishman, still busy with the wheel and not taking his eyes off the binnacle. "Almost overhead but a little to the north. Find the Big Dipper, follow the curve of the handle and the first star you come to of any size is Arcturus." Arcturus then was the huge star that he had seen and it had certainly been visible for Fredericks to take a sight by.

"What about Antares?" asked the priest.

"A little harder," said Moulter. "Look off to the left and you will find three stars in an arc with a rather large buttonhook of stars a little distance away. The best way to find it is don't look too hard. Just sort of gaze, as the old poets used to say, and suddenly it will present itself."

"I can't see it," said Father Bredder.

"Mainsail's in the way. Step aft a bit and take a dekko." The priest went back to the mizzenmast and then readily picked up the figure.

"That's Scorpio," said Moulter. "And that red star in the middle is Antares. Means—rival of Mars. I couldn't resist throwing that piece of information in. I suppose because everybody does."

Father Bredder returned to the cockpit a little puzzled.

"Why the sudden interest in astronomy?" asked the Englishman.

"Just curiosity," said Father Bredder. "Fredericks told me he took a sight that morning—he did not have to further identify the morning—and he used Arcturus and Antares. I wanted to look at them myself."

"Arcturus?" said Moulter. "Well, he knows his business, but Arcturus wouldn't have been my choice. Of course it's big and bright and easy to see. But then it's so high overhead."

"That's a disadvantage?"

"Yes. Also you have to bring the star down through perhaps seventy or eighty degrees to the horizon, and that's a bother. Although, of course, an experienced man like Fredericks would pre-set his sextant and so avoid a lot of the trouble. Still Vega in the north would have given a better cut."

"Perhaps he couldn't get Vega with the spinnaker," said the priest.

"There's Vega now," said Moulter, pointing forward and somewhat to the right. "He could get it beautifully from here. No doubt he had very good reasons for using Arcturus. The horizon below other stars may have been obscured by cumulus. Probably was. I really should not be saying anything, because Fredericks is a topnotch navigator. Still, Arcturus . . . " he lapsed into silence.

"What time did Fredericks take that sight?" asked Storey from the obscurity of the cockpit, where he had been half dozing.

"About five-fifteen. Between five-fifteen and five-thirty," said the priest, who really didn't want to be discussing this at all.

"And you think Sir Harrry went forward belowdecks," continued the New Zealander.

"It is possible," said the priest. "Nobody on the starboard watch which had the duty at that time saw him come on deck. It seems that the only way he could have got on deck unobserved was through that forward hatch."

"Could have been," said the New Zealander. "I thought I heard some kind of scrambling in that sail bin while I was asleep. But I wasn't about to get up and investigate. I figured somebody from the other watch had been sent there to get some sails ready for a change. Larsen said something about going to a smaller spinnaker, but Sir Harry said no. I thought maybe he'd changed his mind and the number two was being gotten out.

"Anyway, I was tired and not going to investigate. I'd had my bellyful of squalls and work during our own watch. So had everybody. I decided to let the starboard watch take care of their own troubles. They'd call us soon enough if we were needed to change spinnakers."

"What kind of a noise was it that you heard?" asked Father Bredder.

"I don't know how to describe it," said Storey. "How do you describe a noise? Look, it was like someone struggling to get a sail bag out of a bin. Kind of grunts and rustles and so on. Those sails are all supposed to be stowed in their own bins, but they never are. They never are on any ship, come

· *139*

to think of it. So you go to the bin for the number two spinnaker and somebody's put the spinnaker staysail there, or the mizzen staysail. And then you hunt around, cussing and pulling at sail bags until you find the one you want. Why the hell is it that nobody ever will put a sail bag back in the right bin?"

"Because if they did, people like Larsen would drop dead from amazement," said Moulter. "And we wouldn't want that. You're probably right, though. Sir Harry and Larsen had a bit of a discussion at the change of watch about going to the smaller spinnaker. And I heard Sir Harry say we were to carry the big one, squalls or no squalls. But he was the type to lie awake thinking about that afterwards. And he may have gone to the sail locker to locate the number two and get it ready for a change. Then he could have the additional pleasure of saying a few sarcastic words about it not being in its place."

"How long did the struggling go on?" asked the priest.

"I don't know," said Storey. "Maybe a minute. Maybe five minutes. I fell asleep in the middle of it."

"Did you hear anybody say anything?"

"No. In fact the noise wasn't very loud. What woke me was some kind of a thump on the bulkhead. Unusual noises always wake me at sea. But then that wasn't so unusual after I'd thought about it. I listened and heard this scrambling and figured it was someone pulling out a sail who lost his footing and fell back against the bulkhead. And then I went to sleep. Probably slept all the better for thinking of the poor bastard struggling."

"Was the light on in the sail locker?"

"I don't know," said Storey. "I didn't get up to look."

"Did anybody else hear this?" asked Father Bredder.

140 ·

Nobody had. And questioned further, all Storey could remember was the bump, a grunt or two and the scraping
sound. He said he had felt rather than heard the bump because his bunk was right next to the bulkhead separating
the stateroom in which the port watch slept from the sail
locker.

The starboard watch slept in another stateroom or really
small cabin immediately aft and this arrangement ensured
that the members of each watch did not disturb each other
unnecessarily. Forward of these two staterooms was the sail
locker and forward of that the quarters for Francis and
Ben, with their own bathroom, cupboards and toilet. Forward of that was the chain lockers, and all these various
compartments were interconnecting. Larsen and Fredericks
each had his own cabin aft near the cockpit whence he
could get on deck in a hurry. And Sir Harry, of course,
lived in the Great Cabin.

"If you weren't sleeping very well, did you hear anybody
pass by your bunk and enter the sail locker, closing the
door behind him?" asked the priest.

"No," said Storey. "You're wrong to think I wasn't sleeping deeply. I was. Somebody passing through and shutting
that door wouldn't wake me because that's a normal noise.
It's only abnormal noises that wake me at sea. I'm like that.
I can be fast asleep and wake up if a sail starts flapping or
just because the motion below isn't right."

"Everybody who has done any sailing gets like that," said
Moulter. "I can sleep right through a change of watch if for
some reason I don't have to go on duty myself. But I'll
wake in a moment if a wave hits the side from the wrong
direction."

"I'd have told you all this before, padre," said Storey,

"but I just didn't think of it. Anyway, you were sleeping not ten feet from me and you didn't hear a thing."

That, Father Bredder reflected, was absolutely true. All had been especially tired by the rigors of the watch which had ended only an hour previously.

"Anyway," said Moulter, "it helps to clear up some of the mystery. It looks like Sir Harry went forward to the sail locker, climbed on deck through the forehatch, and then, missing his footing in the dark, went over the side."

"I don't want to be callous," he continued after a little pause. "But I wonder who gets all that lovely money now? Come to think of it, who gets this lovely big ketch?"

"You know something?" said Storey. "It's an interesting question. But you are a bit of a bastard for bringing it up."

"Just practical," said Moulter, and glanced at his watch in the light of the binnacle. "Your wheel, padre," he said. "Two forty. On the nose."

"Two forty," said the priest, and seated himself behind the helm.

Eighteen

THE FIRST LAND they sighted was the island of Maui. All morning they had been beset by rain squall after rain squall, each thunderous descent of the rain followed by a forty-knot gusting of the wind which lasted for perhaps five or six minutes. Then there was a period of calm and then the northeast trade—very much stronger now than when first encountered—reestablished itself.

It was at the end of one of these purple rain squalls (for that was the color both of the clouds and the air, as the rain thundered down) that Maui was sighted. Yamashito was on deck up forward and he called out, "Haleakala. Fine on the port bow." And there it was, the volcano which to the early Hawaiians had been known as The House of the Sun. It was enormously impressive. It stood a deeper blue above the cumulus, as if some storm cloud had managed to elevate itself so as to lie over the top of the silver fair-weather clouds.

For a few minutes it was impossible to believe that this indeed was land and not just another cloud. And then the property of solidity asserted itself in what seemed to Father Bredder a complete mystical manner. Though he had been only eleven days at sea, nonetheless he was filled with relief and joy at the sight of the land and so were all aboard *Fair*

Maid. Added to the pleasure of landfall was the prospect of escape from the pall of death that lay over the vessel. To be able to get away from this tragedy, to have it reduced in proportion by being once again among hundreds of thousands of their fellows would be a tremendous relief. Ben popped his head up the forehatch and, resting his arms on the deck and standing on the ladder that led from the sail locker, surveyed the volcano with pleasure.

"That cloud, they say, has been there thousands of years—hundreds of thousands of years," he told Father Bredder. "That silvery one that's like a piece of cloth just below the peak. Moves a little, but never disappears. You wouldn't think that something like a cloud could last that long, would you?"

It seemed that Ben knew Maui well. He spoke of a port called Lahaina on the other side of the island that had been a fine place to visit right after the First World War in his early days at sea. "There was a few real Hawaiians around even then," he said. "Never saw such big men anywhere else. Six foot three I'd say and some of them taller. But the women wasn't that pretty. Too fat. Still they was generous, and that's what counts with women. The worst creature on earth is a mean woman—begging your pardon for mentioning it," he added.

Father Bredder chuckled, "No offense at all, Ben," he said.

Ben looked around in that cautious way of his and said, "If we go in closer, we'll have a roaring wind of it for a while. But if we were still racing, this wouldn't be the place to be at all."

"How so?" asked the priest.

"We're too close to Maui. If we were racing, we wouldn't

see Maui. Molokai would be the first sight of land, further to the east. Then down what they call the Molokai Channel, though that ain't its name on the chart, round the point and into Honolulu. That's on Oahu, you know. Some people think Honolulu is an island, but it's just a city on Oahu. Used to be a real nice place, but not any longer."

"What's the matter with it now?" asked Father Bredder.

"Coney Island with coconut palms," said Ben and, having given this poisonous description of one of America's great resort cities, he withdrew down the hatch.

For the next several hours *Fair Maid* skirted the coast first of Maui and then of Molokai, the latter, as seen from the sea, a long and verdant tableland. Course had to be altered to 245 degrees and the sheets hardened in a trifle to fetch Molokai so it seemed that Ben had been right in saying that was not the track that would have been followed had *Fair Maid* still been racing.

Nearing the end of Molokai, he saw to the north a tiny triangle of sail which proved to be *Gesture*. And then out of a rain squall behind *Gesture* and a little further to the north again appeared *Mistral*. The three big Class A boats were still in a position to contend for the finish line. A ripple of excitement ran through the crew of *Fair Maid,* who crowded the decks to look at their rivals.

Moulter, shading his eyes with his hand, said, *"Gesture* has had trouble. She has no mizzen set." Yamashito grabbed a pair of binoculars and confirmed this.

"We could still trim them," said Moulter. "There'll be a set from the north down the channel and *Fair Maid* rides that stuff like a surfboard."

"Hell, we ought to at least try," said Storey. "Sir Harry built this thing to finish first. We owe him that."

Everybody turned to look at Larsen. He was standing at his favorite place, by the mizzen shrouds, wearing that incongruous trilby hat of his. His face was set hard.

He looked aloft at the smooth curve of the main and then to seaward where *Gesture* and *Mistral* fluttered on the waves like two white butterflies. He could see now that both were carrying spinnakers.

They were on the port tack with the wind on their port quarters and intent on making a spinnaker run of it, with a following sea down the wide channel to Diamond Head. He weighed wind and sea and current and the tactical situation of all three boats. He judged, too, the effect of public opinion on his own career and then he said to Moulter, "Give me the staysail inside that Genoa. And send the mizzen staysail up."

The silence that followed was almost a cheer. The crew scurried to get the extra sails up and Larsen told Fredericks to give him a course to clear the end of Molokai by five miles. With all sail set, he then called his two watch captains, Moulter and Smith, back to the cockpit.

"We are in the wrong place," he said. "We are too close to Molokai and when we head for Oahu, we will lose the wind under the lee. So here is what I am going to do." Fredericks brought up a chart and Father Bredder heard Larsen say that they were to have the drifter handy and the small, light-weather spinnaker.

"What about the big one?" asked Smith. "Hell, there's usually thirty knots of wind in that channel."

"Up until four in the afternoon," said Larsen. "When we get there, it wil' be nearer five. The wind will be light. But we can get the sails ready."

146 ·

Father Bredder and Woods went into the sail locker to do this. The sails needed were likely to be the big blue drifter in its tiny bag, the small fair-weather spinnaker, and the big one-and-a-half-ounce spinnaker that ballooned out to a full five thousand square feet. Not only had the sails to be located and put ready on the floor of the sail locker, but also the sheets or lines with which they were trimmed. It took the two of them to handle the big spinnaker, for although it did not weigh a great deal, still it was of an awkward bulk. Woods took the top of the sail bag and Father Bredder the bottom, which had a band of cloth sewn across to form a handle.

When they had the bag in place, Woods opened the top to see that the sail had been properly packed, for unless the head and two clews of the sail were lying available on the top, it would certainly tangle or "hourglass" on the way aloft. Woods didn't like the way the sail was packed when he had the bag open, and after fretting about it for a while decided that with Father Bredder's aid he would repack it.

To do this, the sail had to be taken out of the bag completely and the end of each side located. One side had a border of green cloth sewn down its entire length and the other side a border of red, both to distinguish them from each other and to show which, when the sail was set, should be port and which starboard.

Father Bredder was allotted the port hem of the sail and instructed to fold it carefully in arm lengths working toward the head. He did this while Woods took the starboard side. Then came the problem of getting the sail, thus folded, but still of enormous bulk into the bag which certainly did not look as though it would hold it. Woods told the priest to hold the bag open as best he could and start stuffing the sail in from the center. The priest opened the bag and was about to start this Herculean stuffing job when Woods cautioned him to be sure that the sheets were not lying in the bottom of the sail bag. The priest took a look, saw something in the bottom of the bag which glittered, reached in and took out a small pair of nail clippers.

"For cripes' sake hurry," said Woods. "Holding on to these ends is like waltzing with a bull." Father Bredder stuffed the nail clippers into his pocket and started to pack the sail by armfuls into the bag. Eventually it was all stowed to Woods' satisfaction. "The old way was better," he said. "Send it up in stops with rotten twine. Not much chance of a foul-up. What are you looking at?"

"They're going to need a new spinnaker bag soon," said Father Bredder. "The seam on the bottom here is coming undone."

"Can't help that now," said Woods. "Let's get this positioned. Remember that the starboard side is in its proper place when you have the sail bag facing you and can read the word 'spinnaker' on it. Things like that save a few seconds and that can be important." Father Bredder examined the bag in this position and noted a dark stained area above the word "spinnaker" but said nothing about it.

The two of them located the sheets for the sails, put them where they could be readily got at, and Woods went aft to the cockpit to report all ready. But Father Bredder remained a little while in the sail locker examining the stain and when he came out, he sought out Francis.

"Did Sir Harry have a pair of nail clippers?" he asked.

"No," said Francis. "He never used anything like that."

"Well, just how did he cut his nails?" asked the priest.

"He had a manicure set in a leather case," said Francis. "It's in his cabin. Scissors and nail file. He thought clippers were American. He wasn't too fond of American things."

"I see," said the priest.

"To whom should I pay the money I owe him, now that he's dead?" asked Francis.

"I expect a trustee will be appointed—or perhaps he has an heir," said the priest.

"I was wondering whether I should mention it at all," said Francis. "After all, he is dead. And I don't feel that I owe it to anyone else."

"In a deeper sense, Francis," said Father Bredder gently, "you never really owed it to Sir Harry."

"Oh?" said Francis, surprised.

"No. Legally, of course, you did. But ethically, spiritually, you owed it to yourself. You had stolen from your own trustworthiness—from your own honor. So in paying back you were making good a theft from your own character. When a man steals, he basically steals from himself. It is he who suffers loss—in the sight of God if not in the sight of his fellowmen."

"Oh," said Francis as if he had been shown a point which had only a glancing interest for him. "Still," he added. "With all the money Sir Harry has left, I don't suppose the few hundred dollars I owe could make a difference. I mean if I just didn't pay it back. They wouldn't miss it, would they?"

"No," said the priest. "I am quite sure they wouldn't. They could afford the loss. But that isn't the point. What you have to consider is whether you can afford the loss— the loss of that part of yourself on which no value can be set."

"And what part is that, sir?" asked Francis.

"Your soul," said Father Bredder.

"For a few hundred dollars?" said Francis indignantly.

"For thirty pieces of silver," said Father Bredder, and went on deck.

Nineteen

DIAMOND HEAD lay a little north of true west from the end of Molokai and the compass course, making allowance for deviation and other disturbances, was 265 magnetic. But because he was afraid of being caught under the lee of Molokai and there becalmed—that island ended on its western side in a series of precipitous cliffs—Larsen set his course high and told Smith, who had the wheel, to steer 275. This made a broad reach of it for *Fair Maid* and she had this advantage over *Gesture* and *Mistral,* that they would have to jibe—that is, cross the wind with their stern to round the point to the finish at Diamond Head. But *Fair Maid* had only to fall a little off the wind once she was clear of the lee.

A tingle of excitement now pervaded the whole ship's company. Since the loss of Sir Harry they now had something else to focus their attention on and direct their energies toward. The crew began to race the yacht once more with all the skill at their command.

There being now only a few hours left of the race—Fredericks reckoned two hours forty-five minutes to Diamond Head—there was no question of a watch on duty and a watch at rest. All combined to work the ship under the immediate direction of Moulter, since Smith was at the wheel, and with Larsen as the higher and more remote authority. He stood at his favorite spot by the mizzen shrouds, with that trilby hat clamped on his head, watching not the speedometer nor the wind speed indicator nor the wind direction indicator but the luff of the big Genoa. He seemed to project his mind to the Genoa and mesh or weave his very spirit into the sail so that he could feel the stretch and relaxation of the fibers of the sail with some delicate instrument within him.

"Hold that course, two seventy-five. Don't luff up. Don't fall off," he instructed Smith. "Moulter, get our best men on the Genoa sheets and trim to my order." And so the tremendous sail was not made fast but trimmed with each increase or diminution of the light wind, as if Larsen were sailing, not a seventy-foot yacht but a ten-foot dinghy.

The tactic, exhausting as it was for the crew, paid off handsomely. *Mistral* and *Gesture,* swooping down from the north under their bellying spinnakers, looked for a while as if they would enter the channel well ahead of *Fair Maid*. But then they seemed to slow. Shadows showed through their spinnakers, indicating that the wind was changing or they had hit light airs. *Fair Maid* forged on, slashing through the water and leaving a wake that bubbled behind her like champagne, such was her speed.

When she did slow, it was because they had touched the lee under the cliffs of Molokai, and Larsen altered course five degrees to escape the light wind area. He had only to hold that new course for fifteen minutes to enter the place where the baffled trade winds went from northeast due north, sluicing down the gap between Molokai and Oahu known as the Molokai Channel.

Gesture and *Mistral* to the north were heading about

south-southwest. There was a nasty chop in the channel where the prevailing northeasterly waves ran into a cross sea out of the north caused by the wind shifting in this area. Seas ran together in contrary directions, seething and attempting to cross each other. At times they formed a glittering pyramid of transparent emerald and blue and then exploded, the cascading water leaping easily on board *Fair Maid's* decks.

Yamashito had gone forward with Storey and Woods in case a change of headsails was called for and Father Bredder had been sent to the foremast shrouds and told to stay to windward where his weight would help the ship.

It seemed to the priest that this was calculating in trifles, but then Larsen calculated in trifles and so did Moulter when it came to the pinch. With the priest were Clancy and Todd and Fredericks. Fredericks, however, was working with his sextant. He took sights of the land ahead—the island of Oahu, which emerged blue and gold and green from the low sea glitter and from the angles obtained established the ship's position and its distance off, which information he gave regularly to Larsen.

It was now a little past four in the afternoon. By degrees the wind fell a little lighter and in so doing veered once more from the north to the northeast. The effect on the sea was surprising. In a matter of minutes the chop had gone, the pyramiding and explosion of the waves ceased and the old swell of the northeast trade, a little peaked-up but largely untroubled, prevailed in the channel. Larsen sent for Yamashito, who, being a Hawaiian, knew this channel well.

"The chart says a current northward off Oahu, but nothing this side. Is that so?" he asked.

"There's a very slight south-going current this side of the channel," said Yamashito. "Useful for canoes but not for us."

"What about midchannel?"

"The current heads northwest. It's basically a west-going current that is diverted northward by Oahu. The nearer to Oahu, the more north there is in it. The wind will keep going east, I think. Maybe the spinnaker . . ."

Larsen shook his head. "Not at this time," he said. "It will be after five when we get off Diamond Head. I think we will get a land wind tumbling down off the mountains. Cold mountain air coming down to displace the warm sea air. It will be dead ahead. Or at least ahead of the beam."

Yamashito shrugged.

"You don't think so?" asked Larsen.

"You're the skipper," said Yamashito. "I'd like to have the spinnaker ready. Just in case the wind stays in the east and goes lighter."

"Do that," said Larsen. "Get it up on deck and ready." Yamashito went forward like a cat, and Larsen turned to Moulter. "Detail me two hands to stand by the main and jib halyards as we cross the line. As soon as we are over, I want the halyards started—the sails let slack along the luffs, but not lowered." Moulter looked surprised.

"We must 'scandalize' the sails," said Larsen. "Out of respect for Sir Harry. It is something that should always be done when there is a death at sea." Moulter, despite his attitude of flippancy, was touched. This was the first time he had ever seen any humanity in the sailing master. But then he reflected that Larsen was perhaps thinking of his professional image. He passed the word on to Father Bredder and to Todd, who would undertake this duty.

Larsen was right about the wind. In fifteen minutes it had fallen off to a mere breeze from the east. Five more and all three boats were slopping about in the swell. *Gesture* was in the more miserable position, for she was closer to Oahu when the wind dropped. She, in fact, was swept slowly back up the channel and *Mistral,* who had gained a position slightly ahead of *Fair Maid* but was also closer to the Oahu coast, started turning circles in the water, completely without steerage.

Fair Maid had the advantage of the dying easterly for the longest time. She benefited perhaps by a third of a mile and then she, too, was becalmed in the wallow of the channel but not, like *Gesture* and *Mistral,* being swept to the north.

"How far is *Mistral* from Koko Head?" asked Larsen.

"Seven miles and a fraction—about here," said Fredericks, and gave the location on a plotting sheet. Larsen compared it with the chart and grunted.

"She will get the new wind ahead of us, but she is holding on to her spinnaker."

"Gesture, too," said Fredericks.

"It is not boats now—but skill," said Larsen with some savor.

"And luck," said Fredericks.

"Luck is a bad sailor's name for lack of skill," snapped Larsen.

Moulter said, "We could set the drifter. . . ."

"No," said Larsen. "No drifter. No spinnaker. See the squall on the mountain? That is our wind. Here it comes! Here is the wind!"

The wind struck the other two yachts first. Before the blinding rain that came with the wind cut *Mistral* from view, those on *Fair Maid* saw her spinnaker split. What happened to *Gesture* they could not say, for the rain enveloped *Gesture* and the wind struck at the same time and she disappeared. The squall swooped across the channel, wind and rain, like a charge of cavalry.

The slick water was churned white and came, thus whitened and angered, down on them. A wall of purple like a curtain wiped out the green and gold flanks of the mountains on Oahu and flung down on the boat. Smith, still at the wheel, managed to get her head to fall off a little as the wind struck. For one paralyzing moment *Fair Maid* seemed only to bend before the squall, keeling over and pinned in the water without forward motion. And then she slipped from under the weight of the wind like an orange pip from under a thumb and fled forward, white water over her lee rail, and a quarter wave roaring off her thin stern, angry as a cat.

"The helm," said Larsen and, taking the wheel from Smith, slipped into the helmsman's berth. He did not sit down but stood, one foot against the leeward cockpit coaming and both hands on the big aluminum rim of the steering wheel. He looked for a second at the compass and then back to the sails. The luff of the Genoa he could not see, but he steered by the luff of the main. Visibility was down to a hundred yards, for the rain still pelted down around them—pelted so hard that a mist rose from the decks and the decks themselves were streaming with fresh water which made a considerable pool in the cockpit, for the rain was coming down so hard that the drains, but half open, could not take care of it. Todd opened the drains full so as to get rid of the weight of the water immediately and Moulter, seeing *Fair Maid* so pressed, ordered all hands to the windward rail, he alone remaining in the cockpit to trim the

Genoa on the big winch if need be.

"Diamond Head buoy fine on the port bow," yelled Fredericks, who had been straining to see this mark of the finish line.

"Ease her," yelled Larsen, and Moulter slacked the Genoa sheet a trifle as Larsen put his wheel downwind a little. Suddenly, the rain was gone—gone completely and a blinding sunlight flooded the yacht, the channel and the blue bulk of Diamond Head, now to starboard. Koko Head was already receding and two hundred yards away, but only half a length behind, was *Gesture.* She was making such a slash through the water that she looked like a destroyer going at top speed. Larsen spared her only a glance and returned to his own sails and compass.

"Two seventy-five to the buoy," shouted Frederick. Larsen nodded and, standing steaming in the sunlight, felt the wind drop. He glanced at *Gesture* again. She had fallen off the wind a little to pick up speed. Those aboard, Larsen knew, would be watching him through binoculars, and the binoculars would be focused on his hands.

"Do nothing," he said to Moulter. "I bluff." He yelled for two hands to come back to the cockpit on the run. Back they came and he said, "One take the main sheet, the other behind Moulter on the Genoa. But do nothing at all. Nothing." And then he reached for the bottom of the wheel and with a tremendous swoop of his hands and shoulders went through the motions of putting his wheel downwind to have *Fair Maid* fall off.

The bluff worked. *Gesture,* thinking *Fair Maid* intended to cover her and force her further down the finish line, hardened up into the wind to pass to windward. Too late she realized that *Fair Maid* had not altered course at all,

· *157*

and there was no room for her between *Fair Maid* and the buoy. She fell off the wind again, lost a hundred feet and amid a tremendous blowing of horns and explosion of rockets *Fair Maid* crossed the line—first to finish, which was the job for which she had been built.

"Magnificent," cried Moulter. He seized Larsen's hand and, ignoring the task of steering, pumped it up and down.

"My halyards," cried Larsen. "My halyards. Scandalize my sails, if you please. It is due to the owner."

Father Bredder, Todd and some of the others started the halyards. Wrinkles appeared in the main mizzen and Genoa, which a moment before had been smooth curves of ivory. And with her sails thus bedraggled in the traditional mourning of the sea, *Fair Maid* picked up a tow and, surrounded by a swarm of power cruisers which had been waiting on the other side of the line, headed for the dock in the Ala Wai Yacht Basin.

Twenty

WHILE *Fair Maid* was still at sea and even before the news of the death of Sir Harry Stockton had reached Los Angeles, Captain Normal Redwood, Minardi's chief, had put his bulldozer technique to work on the crew of the yacht. This technique, which Minardi abominated, consisted of amassing in one enormous pile all the information available on the people under investigation—in this instance not only Sir Harry himself, but every member of the ship's company.

This work had kept Minardi and two assistants busy for the whole of the voyage. The two assistants had been increased to five when the news of Sir Harry's death was received. Thus, when *Fair Maid* arrived in Honolulu, Minardi, who had gone out to meet the ship and Father Bredder, had with him a dossier running to four hundred pages of double-spaced typed sheets, complete with fingerprints and photographs, and giving a skeleton biography of every man on board, his field of work, of interest and of travel, and particularly his relationships of any kind with Sir Harry or with the multiple businesses—ranging from copper mining to plastics, with which the knight was connected.

This information had come from the United States, from England, from South Africa, from New Zealand and from

Hawaii itself. And out of this huge mass, after the death of Sir Harry, Minardi had distilled potential motives for murder which might link particular members of the ship's crew to the Englishman's death.

It seemed to him that, given the kind of mentality that will kill (Minardi was of the opinion that not all people could commit murder, even if they had an overwhelming reason for doing so)—given this mentality, at least five of the ship's personnel had sufficient motive for the murder. If it were a murder. On that Minardi had no opinion, and could not make up his mind until he had had a long session on the subject with Father Bredder.

This discussion took place in a suite which Minardi had hired (at his own expense) at the Hawaiian Village Hotel, which had the advantage of being close to the Ala Wai Yacht Basin where *Fair Maid* was berthed. It was also air-conditioned, for the detective suffered miserably from the tropical heat. Father Bredder thought the heat wonderful and could not get over his delight in the blues and greens of the sea, the crisp glitter of the white sand and the lovely deep blue shadow of the palm trees over it.

"It wasn't an accident," said Father Bredder. "Of that I am quite sure. I think, in fact, that I can prove that it wasn't an accident. In the same way that the near-death of Clancy was not an accident. But I have no motives. I don't know enough about the people on board to find a motive. I only know who could have done it and how they could have done it. But why—that I don't know."

"First," said Minardi, removing the filter tip from a king-size cigarette and looking around for matches, "first tell me why you think it wasn't an accident."

"If it was an accident, it leaves too many things unexplained," said the priest. "Larsen thinks that Sir Harry went belowdecks to the forward hatch to satisfy himself about the big spinnaker that the boat was carrying. It was a wild and gusty night. He thinks Sir Harry went up the hatch, slipped on the end of a line lying on the deck and went overboard. Any outcry he made would have been lost in the noise of the sea against the sides of the ship and of the wind in the rigging. So it would have been. I'm quite sure a man could fall overboard in that way and not be missed for a good while."

"And why don't you think it happened that way?" asked Minardi, who, with a little revulsion, had just struck a paper match in the shape of a Hawaiian warrior whose head could be set on fire.

"There's the dressing gown," said the priest. "It went overboard before Sir Harry. At about five in the morning according to the position in which it was found. Who would accidentally drop a dressing gown overboard at such a time? It isn't the kind of garment that would have been left on deck all night—it was an expensive dressing gown. It isn't something that would be torn off the wearer by the wind. So it must have been deliberately put overboard. And the only reason would be to mislead the searchers."

"That's not conclusive," said Minardi. "But I'll accept it for the time being as—well—suggestive."

"Then there's Sir Harry's experience in yacht racing. Larsen says that it's very dangerous for a man to go forward alone and there is an ocean-racing rule on most ships against this. Still, Sir Harry had been in very many races, and he would be aware of such hazards as lines lying around unseen in the dark. He isn't the sort of man who would fall overboard accidentally."

"You'll have to do better," said Minardi.

"It's a case of nothing being sufficient in itself but everything helping," said the priest.

"The next irregularity was the near-death of Clancy." He explained his investigations here and the conclusion that someone had deliberately tampered with the exhaust flange of the generator engine.

"What has that got to do with the death of Sir Harry?" asked Minardi. "It looks like someone was trying to kill Clancy—not Sir Harry—that is, accepting that the leak was deliberately contrived."

"The leak was an accident," he said. "I believe I know how it came about. It came about as part of a plan to kill Sir Harry—to murder him. But the plan was abandoned."

"Murder him in the engine room?" asked Minardi. "Surely he wasn't often in the engine room."

"No. Not in the engine room. But I don't want to explain that now. All I want to do now is to prove that Sir Harry was murdered. I'm saying that somebody attempted to murder him before, but Clancy was almost the victim. I warned Sir Harry, but he did not believe me. He did however try to prevent my investigations into the engine room incident. He said that it was upsetting on the crew and it was only an accident and should not be exaggerated. That attempt to kill Sir Harry failed. It was abandoned, I believe. And then came a second attempt and that succeeded."

"Go ahead," said Minardi. "What else?"

"Then there's Fredericks' navigation. Did you have his sextant checked, as I asked?"

"Yes," said Minardi. "There was what is called an index error of minus three seconds. But that is nothing, for Fredericks was aware of this error and merely added three seconds to his sights and so corrected them. In short, there was nothing wrong with his sextant."

"But his navigation was off," said the priest. "It was off by twenty-three miles—perhaps more. That is the distance that the dressing gown was found south of the ship's position. In other words, Fredericks had stated that the ship was twenty-three miles north of the place where the dressing gown was thrown or fell overboard. That is too big an error to blame on a bad sight or the action of drift and wind on the dressing gown, though Fredericks offered that explanation. It was a deliberate error—in fact, I suspected before Sir Harry was killed that Fredericks was recording a false position—on the ship's chart. Then for reasons that will become clear later, he began to slowly correct that error, starting with the star sight he took the morning Sir Harry went overboard."

"What made you suspicious?" asked Minardi.

"Ghost lights," said the priest. "Both Storey and I one night saw a light appear and disappear south of us. We knew the position of the other ships relative to our own according to Fredericks and none should have been in sight. So I was told that these lights were ghost lights . . . phosphorescence from the back of a series of waves. But they weren't. They were actually the masthead light of *Gesture,* which was at the time within a few miles to the south of us that night, although according to Fredericks she was actually very far away."

"Are you sure that this was not just an error in navigation?" asked Minardi.

"Quite sure," said Father Bredder. "You see the error was sustained from day to day. A competent navigator doesn't keep making an error of twenty-odd miles in his position day after day, unless his sextant is out of order. And Fredericks is a very competent navigator. After we sighted *Mistral* and *Gesture* again off Molokai and the race was resumed, his navigation—or piloting, as it is called in sight of land—was magnificent."

Minardi opened his dossier and turned to the section set off for Fredericks. He mused through it with deliberation and said, while so doing, "Anything else on Fredericks' navigation?"

"Yes," replied the priest. "Sir Harry took a sight once and it differed from Fredericks' position by twenty-five miles. Fredericks tried to make Sir Harry look foolish over this, but I believe Sir Harry's sight was accurate. I began watching Fredericks and he had plenty of opportunity. Even if Sir Harry did fall overboard as Larsen said, Fredericks might have been in a position to shove him. That would depend on the time element."

"There's a motive," said Minardi. "That is, if revenge is a motive. But I don't think it is. Murders, in my experience, are more often preventive killings than judgment killings. That is, people are killed to prevent them doing something and not to equalize things up for something already done. Anyway, putting that aside. If we accept revenge, Fredericks at one time owned about a thousand acres of land in Southern Rhodesia in which one of Sir Harry's mining corporations was interested. Sir Harry's people offered for the land, but Fredericks set a much greater price. Things got very complicated then with suits concerning title and cross suits and stays and orders, and so on. I turned that whole bundle over to our legal department and what came out of it was this: There was no flaw in the original title but there was a flaw somewhere in that the land once was owned by a non-national and Fredericks' title derived through the non-national. Non-nationals of certain racial groups cannot legally own land in this part. Fredericks, defending his title, had to borrow on the land. And the result is an old story. His title was upheld, but he owed so much money in defending the title that his creditors took the land in settlement of his debts and then Sir Harry's company bought the land—at a little below the original offer, from the creditors. It's a perfectly legal piece of business and something of the sort goes on all the time. But Fredericks made the usual remark that one day he would get Sir Harry—a remark that I would probably have made myself in the circumstances."

"So, if revenge would be a motive, then we have a motive for Fredericks."

Father Bredder nodded agreement. "The trouble is," he said, "that Fredericks didn't do it. He intended to kill Sir Harry. And he tried. But he didn't succeed."

"He tried?"

"Yes. He's a good navigator, but he bungles elsewhere and he bungled the murder attempt. What he proposed to do, I think, was to pump or divert exhaust gas from the generator into Sir Harry's Great Cabin through the drain in the shower. I was puzzled for a while about a black smudge in the drain, but I think that is what it was—carbon from the generator exhaust. Fredericks was one member of the crew who could be about at all times without any questions asked. It would not be hard for him to get into the engine room at night and by disconnecting the exhaust line going through the hull and hooking it up to the drain from Sir Harry's shower, divert the carbon monoxide into Sir Harry's cabin. All those lines were standardized on *Fair Maid,* so that fittings were interchangeable. I think if the system is examined, something of that sort will be found. I checked the exhaust myself, but beyond finding that it had been tampered with, I found no connection with the drain from the shower. He made the connection and had a trial run and then changed his mind in a panic and so restored everything to normal."

"I should think he did change his mind," said Minardi. "Carbon monoxide poisoning is very easy to identify."

"If the body were found," said Father Bredder. "I believe what he intended to do was make the hookup in the afternoon so that the carbon monoxide gas would enter the Great Cabin about eight in the evening when Sir Harry usually rested for a while after dinner. It would be dark then, you know. And he planned not to kill Sir Harry but have him come on deck, in a groggy state, to get fresh air. He would be expecting him to come up, and would push him over the side. If he didn't come up, he would go to his cabin and get him up. And then the false position he would report when it was discovered that Sir Harry was not aboard, would make it practically certain that the body was not found."

"That's an elaborate murder plan," said Minardi. "Too elaborate. It calls for a mechanical hookup made at a particular time, for the victim being in a particular place, and for the victim, half dead with carbon monoxide poisoning, to leave that place and then coming on deck to be pushed overboard by the killer who is waiting for him to appear."

"Yes," agreed Father Bredder. "It is elaborate and for that reason Fredericks abandoned it. But in restoring the piping he did not make a gas-tight joint at one flange in the exhaust and the result was that Clancy was nearly killed. He was using a crescent wrench to tighten the nuts and bolts and the wrench slipped. He didn't get one bolt tight."

"Why use a crescent with all kinds of wrenches available?" asked Minardi.

"Because he couldn't see well close up," said the priest. "He used a magnifying glass to read the tables of figures in the *Nautical Almanac*. I know because I borrowed the magnifying glass from him. He wasn't able to read the sizes on the various wrenches available. A crescent was the answer. The jaws of crescents work open after a little use. It slipped on the last nut he had to tighten."

"Having failed that way, assuming it was Fredericks," said Minardi, "why couldn't it have been Fredericks who finally did murder Sir Harry?"

"Because if he did," said the priest, "he would never have thrown that dressing gown overboard separate from the body. You see the dressing gown clearly showed that Fredericks was cooking his navigation. It gave an actual location for *Fair Maid* different from the plotted location given by Fredericks. And when Sir Harry *did* go overboard, Fredericks was actually correcting his navigation so as to finally arrive at the ship's true position. No. Fredericks planned murder and perhaps even attempted murder—though I don't suppose we can prove that. But he didn't actually kill Sir Harry."

"Then who did?" asked Minardi.

"It comes down to someone who could throw Sir Harry overboard in daylight without arousing suspicion," said Father Bredder.

Twenty-one

BARBARA MINARDI arrived the following day and her arrival was another reason why her father had, at his own expense, taken such luxurious quarters in the Hawaiian Village Hotel. She had not come out with the lieutenant because there was something she had to do in Los Angeles that could not be done until a week after he left. She would not explain what this something was, and in any case, with the worry of the investigation on his hands, he was content for Barbara to stay with friends for a few days until he had control of affairs in Honolulu.

She arrived on a Saturday, full of excitement and pleasure, pretty and vivacious and at sixteen all woman and all child, wise and innocent. She was delayed a little at the airport by the agricultural inspectors and Minardi, waiting for her behind the barrier, said impatiently, "That girl could find trouble anywhere. I was able to walk straight through. She probably has a sack of old apples that she won't be parted from for one reason or another."

But when Barbara finally got through and flung herself into her father's arms as if they hadn't seen each other for a century, and told him he looked pale and ought not to wear reddish ties, all his impatience was gone and he was surprised to find himself promising to take her on a picnic and sightseeing tour of the island the following day, which was Sunday. So they left the airport, Barbara holding the arms of both men and chatting away with such vivacity and excitement that Minardi could not remember where he had parked his car and Father Bredder could not get a word in edgeways. The picnic having been decided upon, he had one favor to ask, however—and that was that Ben, the cook on *Fair Maid,* be allowed to join the party.

"He was a friend of mine on board," said the priest in explanation. "One way and another, I think I owe quite a lot to Ben."

"A sea cook?" cried Barbara. "How marvelous. I don't want to be corny, but I don't suppose he's got a parrot."

"No," said the priest. "But he's got a fund of stories that might put him in the same league with Long John Silver."

When Ben accepted the invitation, he was quite speechless. He seemingly rarely received any shore invitations when his ship was in harbor. Indeed, he was very nervous and spoke about shopping for clothes, and the priest was hard put to persuade him that the whole thing about a picnic was that what you wore was of no importance.

"Well," said Ben. "There's one thing I can do. I can fix the lunch. Seeing that you have been kind enough to ask me along, I can certainly do that." And fix the lunch he did. He spent the whole of the afternoon baking bread for sandwiches, and making a potato salad with his own mayonnaise, and a fruit salad, and he made a special filler for some of the sandwiches of shredded raw fish and a touch of horseradish that Barbara described as "out of sight"—a description that perplexed Ben mightily.

Father Bredder was up before dawn, for he had been promised an opportunity of saying his Mass in a small church some distance from Honolulu and on the coast. It was the kind of church he especially loved—simple and made of stone, with plastered walls. The statue of Christ had a lei of blossoms around the neck, and the old wooden pews smelled not of varnish or furniture polish but of flowers and incense. He offered up his Mass for his friend Ben, and was so taken by the church and the little bay on which it stood that he suggested they have their picnic there, and this suggestion was approved by everybody.

Ben had contrived to get some clothes for the picnic. He had somehow, despite his baking and preparing of food, got down to the shops at Waikiki and bought a truly magnificent Hawaiian shirt of scarlet and silver, all flowers and dancing girls. And he had bought a lei of tiny seashells for Barbara, an ashtray with the arms of Hawaii on it for Minardi, and a pair of nail clippers for Father Bredder and himself.

"You and me has got to be specially careful with our hands," he said. Barbara had also done some shopping for, although she had just arrived, it seemed that she had brought very little luggage, being determined to get everything she needed in Honolulu. Among the sun dresses and culottes and sunbonnets were three pairs of men's swimming trunks and an enormous plastic bottle of sun tan lotion.

"None of you," she said, "would have remembered to buy those."

The picnic was a great success, all the greater, rather to Minardi's surprise, because Ben was along. It was he who warned them against walking barefoot under the tamarinds which shed inch-long thorns into the silky sand to pierce their feet. And it was Ben who, without being in the slightest degree officious, collected some thick green leaves to be rubbed on arms, legs and back as a mosquito repellent. The bread he baked was so good that it reminded Father Bredder of pre-atomic Ohio, and Minardi compared it to the village bread of Sicily.

"It will probably make me fat," said Barbara, "but I've got hundreds of years to get slim again." She wanted to explore after lunch and went off with her father while Ben and Father Bredder tidied up the picnic fragments.

"When you're getting on, like I am," said Ben, watching Minardi and his daughter walking down the beach, "it makes you feel good to see something like that. I've seen a lot of things in my life, as I expect you have, sir. But something like that is among the best of them."

Ben could not be cured of calling Father Bredder "sir" nor Minardi either. The priest decided that this represented an attitude that belonged to him and without which he would be unhappy. He was very fond of Ben, but there was something he had to say that wrenched him.

"Ben," he said. "When did you lose your nail clippers?"

"I'm not going to lie about it," said Ben. "Not to you anyway, sir. It was the night I got rid of Sir Harry. I think I dropped them in that spinnaker bag when I was putting him in there. I suppose you found them?"

"Yes, Ben, I did," said the priest. His heart was so heavy that it was only with greatest difficulty that he could get himself to ask the next question.

"You killed him, didn't you, Ben," he said.

"Yes," said Ben. "I did." He looked at the priest and the misery on Father Bredder's face upset him so much that he reached out his hand and patted the priest on the shoulder.

"Don't let it worry you, sir," he said. "It was something

· *171*

that had to be done. It wasn't something that there wasn't any choice about. And it couldn't wait, either. So since it had to be done, why, I did it, as a seaman should. I've learned that much about life. Only harm comes of putting things off that you don't want to do. So the best thing is just face up to them and do them."

"How did you do it, Ben?" asked the priest. "I think I know. But I'd sooner you told me."

"I'll tell you right away," said Ben. "But there's one thing I want to make clear if I can. I killed him, all right, but I wasn't out of my mind. I was quite sane and I'm quite sane now. If I'd been out of my mind then I wouldn't perhaps have killed him. What I'm trying to say, sir, is that killing Sir Harry was the most sensible thing I've done in my life. I did it on purpose and I expect I'll be executed for it. That's the way the law is and it can't be changed for me and I don't expect it to be. But when it comes to trial, I don't want anybody pleading insanity for me because that would take away the whole reason for killing him."

Father Bredder said nothing to this and Ben went on with his explanation.

"As for how I killed him, sir, I'm sure you know that yourself. I threw him overboard, and he drowned. Here's the way it was. I'd made up my mind that he had to be killed and I'd formed my plan for how to do it. All I needed then was the opportunity.

"Now that morning Francis, who bunks with me up forward, had been wakened to get Sir Harry a cup of coffee around five o'clock, as you know. Francis woke me with his noise when he got back and I was just getting off to sleep again when I heard someone in the sail locker which, as you know, is just next to our bunkroom. I went to see who it was, half suspecting that it might be Sir Harry—he was always prowling around, as you know—and of course it was.

"I asked him if he needed anything and he told me he didn't and to get back to bed. He was a bit sharp as always. He started up the ladder leading through the forehatch to the deck and when he had both hands on the side of the ladder, knowing this was my chance, I hit him with my blackjack."

"You carry a blackjack?" asked Father Bredder.

"Ever since I got that job on the lumber schooner in Seattle," said Ben. "The cook who had the job before me and got drunk, he looked me up one day and worked me over, and ever since then I got a blackjack. People say carrying a blackjack is bad and then they go out and study karate and spend a lot of money doing it. A blackjack doesn't cost a dollar and is better than all that Japanese stuff. Anyway, as I say, I hit him and he tumbled down without any trouble at all. You learned to use a blackjack right in Seattle in the old days. That and a seaman's belt with a heavy brass buckle on the end. It was part of sailoring.

"Well, there he was unconscious on the floor and I knew he would stay that way for a while, for I hit him hard. In fact, I was afraid I had hit him too hard and if he was found he might be dead not of drowning but concussion. So I stuffed him in the spinnaker bag—we were flying the big one and left him there and told Francis to give me his dressing gown. I expect that's when I lost my nail clippers out of my shirt pocket."

"So Francis had the dressing gown?" asked Father Bredder, ignoring this.

"Yes, he had," said Ben. "It had gold buttons on it and he was going to cut them off and substitute them with some others that weren't gold, but looked very like them. Those buttons were shaped like balls, you know, so the shape wouldn't give him away. Anyway, I told him to give me the dressing gown and I took and threw it over the side, going up the forehatch where I could see Mr. Fredericks was busy at his sextant."

"You went on deck to throw it overboard?" asked Father Bredder.

"No," said Ben. "That wasn't necessary. I just opened the hatch and waited until she rolled and threw it and it went over without a hitch. When you've been cooking on boats awhile, you get a lot of experience at that.

"Then I came down and told Francis about Sir Harry. He was frightened. He hasn't any more courage by nature than a hen in a rainstorm. But I pointed out that if we dumped Sir Harry over the side, everybody would say it was an accident. We would neither of us be suspected. And he wouldn't have to keep robbing Sir Harry to pay his gambling debts."

"Gambling debts?" said Father Bredder.

"I expect he said it was his daughter," said Ben. "So it was in the beginning. But to get money for that he stole and he gambled, and lately he had gambling debts to pay as well as what he owed Sir Harry. Gambling debts are the worse sort, because people you owe money to gambling get it—or else.

"In the end he agreed. We took Sir Harry out of the sail bag and put him in the big garbage can and put some garbage over the top and then it was just a matter of throwing him overboard at the usual time."

"Weren't you afraid that someone might open the garbage can?" asked the priest.

"No," said Ben. "That's one thing you never have to be afraid of—nobody wants to take the top off a garbage can at sea. Only the cook. We threw the garbage overboard in daylight as we always did and Sir Harry with it. I just waited for a squall when everybody was trying to keep out of the rain and dumped him, and lucky I did, because he was beginning to come around. And then all that was needed was for Francis to get his breakfast and report that he could get no reply from his cabin and look concerned about it. And Francis is good at looking concerned."

"Why did you throw the dressing gown overboard?" asked the priest.

"Well, it gave a chance of misleading the searchers if it was found, and there was bound to be a search," said Ben. "You see it's this way. If a man is found floating in the ocean dead, then the doctor that examines him may look to see if there's water in his lungs and say he drowned and leave it at that. But with an important man like Sir Harry, the doctor might look him over a bit close. And though a blackjack don't leave much of a bruise, it leaves some. So I would be better off if he weren't found. The dressing gown would throw everybody off about the place he went overboard."

"Why did you wait until daylight, Ben?" said the priest.

"Well, to get farther from that dressing gown, for one thing, and because I always dump the garbage in daylight," said Ben. "If I done it before daylight, it would have been odd. But you haven't asked me why I did it, and that's the most important thing."

"Why did you do it, Ben?" asked the priest.

"Well, it wasn't because of my sister," said Ben. "And it wasn't because I was what they call mentally unsound—nothing like that at all. I didn't like my sister. She wasn't a very nice woman. She was hard on her husband, who had been a shipmate of mine on those lumber schooner days. She had soon wasted the money he saved and I was not at all sorry when I heard that she had been killed by Sir Harry in England."

"Killed by Sir Harry in England?" echoed Father Bredder.

"Edna Phillips. His housekeeper," said Ben. "But then perhaps you wouldn't know about that. She died in her room of gas poisoning. I had had a letter from my sister written two weeks before that. She had complained about the gas in her room. Said the stove was forever out of order and being repaired. She was always complaining anyway, so I paid no attention. She said in that letter that she had been told there would be no gas for her stove for a month and she would have to make her cup of tea and other things during the night on a spirit stove.

"Now my sister was a very careful woman about things like turning off the gas and turning off taps and lights and so on. A hard woman to live with. And I'm sure that she always turned off that gas to the stove in her room—when there was gas laid on. But since there wasn't going to be any for a month, maybe she got careless and didn't notice that the valve on the stove was left open. And then all that was necessary was to let the gas come through the stove for a little while at night and she would have died an accidental death. Only it wasn't accidental. Not that I minded in the case of my sister. She was just a stumbling block for decent people in a hard world, and better out of it."

"Ben," said Father Bredder. "That's all speculation. And there isn't any reason at all why Sir Harry would want to kill your sister."

"Except that it was a hobby," said Ben. "It made him feel clever to kill people in what looked to everybody like accidents but were really planned. And then, as you say yourself, no motive could ever be found. Like there would be no motive for a man in Sir Harry's position in the world to kill someone like my sister. Or his chauffeur. Or that gardener feller. Of course there was a motive as I have said in that it was his hobby. But police always look for a motive for killing a particular person. And Sir Harry didn't have a motive for any particular person—any more than a sportsman has a motive for shooting a particular bird. It's a hobby, like I said."

"Go on," said Father Bredder grimly.

"I'm glad you believe me when I say that I didn't hold anything against Sir Harry for killing my sister," said Ben. "She was a nasty piece of work. But that chauffeur and gardener. That was a different matter. And then when the rigger fell and was killed—right after Sir Harry had been up the same mast in the same bosun's chair. And then again Clancy. Only he didn't die. Well, I thought something ought to be done about it."

"Like what?" asked Father Bredder, though he knew the answer.

"Like it had to be stopped," said Ben. "The police would never stop it. They couldn't stop it. An accident is an accident. And the first question the police ask, if you say murder, is, 'What's the motive?' Am I right, sir?"

"The police were investigating Sir Harry," said Father Bredder. "He was being watched. Some things turned up about the death of the rigger that looked suspicious. The spring in that snap hook used by the rigger had been tampered with. The bolt would seat properly only if closed by hand—not with the spring closing it. That is perhaps why Sir Harry escaped but the rigger fell to his death. (Minardi had told him of this.) These things were under investigation. If what you say is true, Sir Harry would eventually have been found out."

"Ah, but by then it would have been too late," said Ben. "He would have killed again. Someone else, see? Someone he *had* to kill this time. It would have been different this time because he would have had a motive to kill a particular person. But it would have looked like an accident. You can be sure of that."

"Who had he to kill?" asked Father Bredder.

"Why, you," said Ben. "You were on to him. You'd been investigating that accident to Clancy that wasn't an accident. So you were next on the list. I tell you, sir, if Sir Harry hadn't gone overboard, you would have. And no man would have been able to say anything about it except that you'd stumbled or slipped and you wasn't an experienced hand and it was only to be expected.

"Sir Harry had found a new sport that was better than mountain climbing or ocean racing—killing people by accident. It was a proper sport because it had its rules, see. The most important rule was that you had to kill someone doing something at which they were expert—like my sister knew all about gas stoves and turning them off. And that chauffeur knew all about jacking up cars. And that rigger knew all about going up in bosun's chairs. And Clancy knew all about the engine." Father Bredder was about to interrupt to say that Clancy's near death had nothing to do with Sir Harry. But he had not the heart to do so then.

"Of course killing you wouldn't have been part of the sport," continued Ben. "Because it wouldn't fit into the rules. But I knew you were next and I knew you wouldn't reach Honolulu if Sir Harry wasn't dealt with. So I did what I had to, and I expect to pay for it. But at my time in life, that doesn't matter so much. Even before I did it, I thought about being executed. And the only bad thing about being executed is that you know you're going to die then, instead of just knowing that you're going to die sometime. But that don't trouble me. Just so long as they know I was sane and did what a sane man had to do."

"Why doesn't it trouble you?" asked Father Bredder gently.

"Because I'm a sailor," said Ben. "Every voyage is like dying a little, see? You're leaving places you know and people you know, and although you think you know where you're going, you can't ever be sure you'll get there, the ocean being what it is. So I'm used to it and I'll shove off as usual when they let go my lines."

"You killed him to save my life?" the priest asked.

"Yes," said Ben. "Like I said, you were next. And I had an extra-special reason for saving you. You gave me your blessing when I asked for it. Remember? Nobody ever blessed me before."

Twenty-two

EVERBODY WAS subdued on the journey back, except Ben. Barbara and Minardi were tired by the sand and the sea and Minardi was so sleepy he could scarcely keep his eyes open. Barbara was tired, too, and in one of her reflective moods. Father Bredder was driving and Barbara sat beside him so her father could snooze in the back. The priest caught Barbara looking at him once or twice with eyes that were too wise for sixteen and once she said to him, "You keep sighing. You shouldn't, you know. It's bad for the heart."

"I didn't know that," said Father Bredder.

"Well, it isn't in biology or anything else, but every time you sigh it wrings a drop of blood from your heart and that's bad for it." But she didn't ask him what he was sighing about. Once she turned around and, looking straight at Ben, said, "The picnic was lovely. It was really the nicest I've ever had."

Father Bredder realized that Barbara was for some secret reason being very grownup. Ben was overcome with pleasure at the success of his cooking and even began singing a little song, not of the sea, but about a man called Crazy Jack who had been, it seemed, captain of a wagon team. Father Bredder had made up his mind to tell Minardi about

Ben sometime later—he couldn't say when. He wished he could delay it until Barbara had gone back to California. But that was impossible.

As matters turned out, delay was not necessary.

They were to leave the car at the Ala Wai Yacht Basin, and the priest pulled into the side of busy Ala Moana Boulevard to get out with Ben and hand over the car to Minardi. Barbara opened her door, which was close to the sidewalk, and got out and Father Bredder slipped under the wheel and out the door. But Ben, a sailor ashore, stepped out into the millrace of the traffic.

There was a blaring of horns from several cars. A taxi swerved and missed Ben by inches and then an empty pineapple truck hit him and he flipped into the side of the rented car and then back from it and in a moment was a limp heap on the pavement, with a dark pool spreading below him.

Minardi grabbed Barbara and, pressing her head against his chest, turned her quickly away. Father Bredder was on his knees in a moment beside Ben. Another truck had stopped and created a space of safety in which the priest knelt. He was no stranger to death and he knew that Ben was dying. He prayed the ancient prayers for mercy and forgiveness and made over him the sign of the cross which is the sign of the love of God. And then Ben said in a whisper that the priest had to bend down to catch,

"You all right, sir?"

"Yes," said the priest.

"Thank you for the blessing, then." And so he died.

The whole crew of the *Fair Maid* and many from other ships of the Transpac attended the funeral of the sea cook. Francis was there too, though under arrest. But Minardi arranged for him to come.

· *181*

It was a very simple funeral service, given by Father Bredder at the little church at which he had said Mass, and remarkable in only one thing—that was that Ben, in his coffin, held in his hands one rather small orange. Some thought that this had something to do with him being a cook. But Barbara, who had with difficulty brought the orange through the plant inspection at Honolulu, and Father Bredder, who had raised it, knew that it was a gift of love that might, perhaps, be marked in heaven.